GW01159466

Tides of Love Rhythms of Passion

Tides of Love: Military

Lilly Grace Nash

Published by JL Lam Publishing, 2024.

TIDES OF LOVE RHYTHMS OF PASSION

First edition. October 20, 2024.

Copyright © 2024 Lilly Grace Nash.

ISBN: 979-8227115355

Written by Lilly Grace Nash.

Also by Lilly Grace Nash

Courting Justice
Alliances & Betrayals
The Billionaire's Legal Affair
Objection to Love
Love's Final Exoneration

SEALs of Love Romance
Undercover Hearts
Fractured Hearts
Healing Hearts

Second Chance Romance
Damaged Ex-SEAL's Second Chance
Ex-SEAL's Second Chance

Tides of Love: Military

Tides of Desire A Soldier's Canvas
Tides of Love Rhythms of Passion

Standalone
Billionaire's Nanny Fake Marriage
Silent Hearts, Secret Desires
Boss Daddy's Nanny

Watch for more at https://jllampublishing.com/
lilly-grace-nash.

Table of Contents

To my beloved husband,

whose unwavering support, endless encouragement, and steadfast belief in me have been the guiding light throughout my journey.

Your love is the foundation upon which I build my dreams.

The Siren's Song

Jarrett

Jarrett grew up enchanted by his grandfather's tales of military glory. So at 18, he enlisted - drawn to prove the mettle of his Wyoming rancher bloodline. He earned his Green Beret quickly and thrived for over a decade leading ops around the globe. Though each successful mission left deeper scars etched into his psyche.

His latest tour in Afghanistan had started routine. Clearing operations along the remote Pakistan border to disrupt Taliban trafficking networks. Nights huddled around the patrol base swapping stories and cigarette butts with his tightknit ODA squadmates.

But late one night the base came under coordinated mortar attack. Scrambling through the chaos as explosions rocked the earth, Scrambling through the chaotic mortar attack, Jarrett rallied his squad to reinforce the north guard tower. But searing shrapnel tore through the structure's sandbag walls first. He watched helplessly as young Private Hartman collapsed mere steps ahead - the last friendly face Jarrett would see his brothers-in-arms make before the rest was obscured in smoke and blood. The next few weeks bled feverish battles to beat back emboldened Taliban ambushes. When the dust finally settled, alive but diminished, Jarrett's ODA flew stateside heavy with unfinished business.

The tarmac view back home foretold only cold isolation ahead. Until twists of fate guided Jarrett's weary boots towards an empty corner bar one night...and the siren song that would change everything.

Another deployment done, another brother lost. The plane ride stateside was spent staring numbly out the window, replaying the ambush that took Hartman from us. His screams still echoed in my dreams. Some of the guys headed straight for the nearest bar as soon as we touched down. Can't blame them. But solitude called to me after months of packing into tight quarters with nothing but swaggering men.

I found myself wandering the New Orleans early spring streets alone, finally able to breathe, bracing against the chill. My wandering led me past an old corner bar. Muffled piano music fluttered out the windows, bluesy, like smoked honey. I ducked inside, drawn instinctively towards its promise of warmth.

The joint was empty save the bartender nodding off to a basketball game's muted colors on TV. And there she was, tucked away in the back nook – an angel bathed under low lights, fingers dancing passionately over the black and white keys. Her voice spun silken but full of ache when she sang. Safe to say she had me under her spell soon as our eyes locked.

"She doesn't mess with the punters. Sorry, but you wouldn't be the first to be disappointed." The bartender smiled in a way that wasn't obnoxious, it really was sorrow. I think he'd tried once or twice and had been cut down. "What's her name?"

"Antoinette."

I liked the sound of that, and I told him that I was sorry that he didn't get far, but I was going to try. He shrugged, "Can't blame ya, but you look like an excitable guy. Didn't want you thinking that it was you." I ordered my drink and waited for him to get it.

His words were prominent in the front of my head, while I downed the drink and got another. The music stopped and a husky voice was heard through the microphone I hadn't noticed before and my desire to meet her had gone full tilt. That voice!

She stood up and I watched her turn around like it was in slow motion. Porcelain skin, red lips, curved frame. Antoinette was everything that I was looking for tonight and probably for the rest of my life. She was the sort of woman that I saw and at once wanted to claim her. I didn't know the first thing about her, but it didn't matter. She was beautiful and made heavenly sounds, which was all I needed to know to want to pursue her.

Since the bartender warned me that she wasn't interested in regular patrons, I couldn't jump her from the beginning. I wanted to walk right up to her, claim her with a kiss and throw her over my shoulder and take her with me. I couldn't do that, but just the thought of it had me tightening in my pants. I hope this chick has a thing for soldiers.

I lucked out first because she sat down right next to me. Antoinette didn't say anything, ordered a drink and took several sips, before I turned to her and told her that she sounded amazing. I wanted to compliment her talent first, so that when I talked about her looks later it wouldn't seem so shallow. She likely knew that she was a ten.

"Thank you for your kind words." Antoinette barely looked at me, focused more on the drink in front of her. "Did the bartender tell you that I wasn't interested?"

I wasn't ready for the question or the intense green eyes that met mine. "Something like that."

She giggled, "I bet he's mad that you still chose to go that route. Jimmy thinks that we are going to be together one day. I have told him it isn't going to happen, he's just not my type."

I perked up, "Does that mean that you are interested in seduction?"

She almost spit her drink out in a very delicate manner when I said that. She wasn't expecting me to be blunt, but the second whiskey made it easier to say what I meant. I wanted her and Antoinette was not playing the innocent girl that didn't want to be harassed.

"I do have a thing for the uniform, and you wear it better than anyone that I've ever seen."

I was shocked by her own words. She wasn't at all what I expected. "Do you want to get out of here?" It was the first thing that came to mind, even if it was a little premature.

Antoinette scoffed, "I have a little while longer on the clock, but if you aren't wasted by the time I get off, maybe."

I looked at the empty glass and while I had fully planned to get blasted, being with Antoinette for the night sounded far better. She had given me all the incentive that I needed to stay sober, "Not another drink."

She smiled and finished hers. "Any requests?"

My mind went to an image of her on her knees, but she laughed and that, at once, stopped my line of thought. "A song. Do you have any requests for a song?"

I nodded, "Play our song again."

Antoinette was confused and I sang a few notes that stuck in my head. She agreed and told me the name, but I wasn't even paying attention. I saw her lips moving and then the smile before she walked away. The night had certainly taken a turn and I can't say that it was one for the worse. With Antoinette in my arms, I'm sure that I will be able to forget everything.

***

We stepped out into the chilly night, still laughing. Something about being with Antoinette made me feel free - like she saw the man behind the uniform. I reached for her hand and she took it, eyes sparkling. The bartender watched knowingly as we left.

We strolled quiet streets under streetlamps. I led her towards the little bungalow I'd rented on leave. Her hair tumbled in the gentle breeze as we walked. I savored how she felt nestled close as I guided us through sleeping neighborhoods.

Walking up the gravel drive, I ascended the steps and paused at the door. She gazed expectant up towards where candlelight flickered the bedroom window. No assumptions, only longing that tonight our bond might deepen beyond confinement of words and wine shared.

I fumbled the key, suddenly self-aware of war's imprint scarred upon me. Would this angel embrace man and soldier alike? The deadbolt's click sounded deafening loud as I held the door to behold what together we'd uncover.

Antoinette was looking around my place. We had just got through the door, and I tried to see it through her eyes, but I was far more interested in the woman in front of me. She looked nervous, purse clasped tightly in her hand. "Would you like something to drink?"

"Not really. I already feel like I'm buzzed around you."

I felt the same way, my body was running on a different frequency and though I'd never felt this way before, I certainly liked the feeling of it. She was still standing in the foyer, unsure, so I did the one thing that we'd been dancing around the whole night. I leaned down and gently kissed her. It was immediate the desire that came over me and I pulled her in closer to feel the curves I could see in her tight dress. The dress was worn to get attention and it certainly had mine all night.

She gasped as I picked her up. "Let's take this somewhere more comfortable."

Antoinette agreed and we kissed as I took her into the bedroom. I wanted her horizontal and on my bed. There was not even a moment of her being unsure now, swept away like I was. I wanted to keep her clinging to me in need. I had questions, wanted answers, but her body writhing in my arms naturally trumped everything else.

I laid her down, covering her with my own body. I didn't want to let go, not even long enough to get us both undressed. I was shaking inside with desire, and it was only when she kept lifting her hips and grinding on me that I could get the respite that I so desperately needed. Her dress was off in moments, leaving me everything to see and take in. I memorized every line and curve, touching some of them with a light finger that made her shiver. I told her how beautiful she was, but Antoinette didn't need to hear it.

"You have too much on."

I started to go for the shirt, but Antoinette shook her head. "Let's leave that on."

I didn't say anything. She'd already admitted that the uniform was doing something for her. It was likely why she said yes as quickly as she did. Whatever the reasoning for her to be in my arms, I was going to take it, even if it had nothing to do with me. The pants came off and the shirt covered up too much, so Antoinette changed her mind and started to unbutton it while I moved back over her. She looked between our bodies and saw my hard length ready to go and gasped. "Here I was thinking that you were going to need some encouragement. That I would have to touch and taste you a bit," Antoinette teased. If I wasn't inches from pushing deep, maybe I would have gone for that, but there was no way that I could take it now.

Her small hands worked to get my shirt unbuttoned and her hands moved to my chest at once. "Maybe I should've let you take this off too." She mumbled it more to herself, but that was enough of a hint for me. I wanted the shirt off, simply so that she wanted me, not the uniform. It was a silly distinction, but one I wanted to be clear.

Antoinette's fingers glided over my muscles as I came back to on top of her. Her legs opened with very little encouragement. I could see that she wanted me, the heavy draw was there, and I don't think either one of us could help it. Her arms encircled my neck as she pulled me down for a kiss. The rest of me naturally moved downwards and her wetness let me slide right in. She called out into my mouth, my lips muffling the sound.

I wasn't all the way in, before I pulled my mouth off of her. "Oh my God." She was so wet, so hot, I was going to lose it right there, I was sure of it. This was heaven.

I looked down to her glittering eyes and her hips rose up to take me deeper, her eyelids close. I saw her lips purse and tried my best to focus on something else, anything else. I had to fight the immediate urge to fill her full of my seed, something that I'd never had a problem with before.

Antoinette's moans and movements made me push through the feeling and start thrusting. She obviously wasn't going to take no for an answer, so I had to grit my teeth and push deeper. If I made long, fast strokes, it took her breath away and she stopped moving for a moment. That was the only way that I was going to be able to go forward, without losing it right then and there.

Her gaze met mine and she urged me to go faster with her nails digging into my ass. She was so close, told me so and I pushed her over the edge as my own need tried to come to a head. I couldn't let it happen.

The sounds that came from her sent me over, whether I held on for dear life or not. Antoinette got the better of me and I couldn't stop it from happening. I cursed under my breath as I filled her with my hot seed.

I stayed like that for several moments, still deep and throbbing inside of her. Antoinette pushed back on my chest and made me realize that it had been a while. I could have stayed there forever. As soon as my cock met the cool air of my room, I wanted to go right back in. With a soft push, Antoinette made it clear that she needed a few moments. I didn't blame her, I'd lost myself for a moment there. We laid on our back, catching our breath.

While I watched her chest rise and fall, I could only grow with need. Antoinette looked over at me and then at what was now hard and throbbing again. "You've been gone a while, huh?"

I wanted to agree, have a reason for it acting this way, but I wasn't given time to stumble over an answer. Antoinette moved to cover my body with hers and I knew then that she really was the girl of my dreams. She whispered my name as she settled down on top, not stopping her slow descent until I'd disappeared inside of her. I waited for her eyes to reopen, before gripping her hips and pushing up. The sound as she went deeper, was one I would never care to get out of my ears. I could focus on nothing else, and it became a game, how many times could I make Antoinette moan in such a way. It was musical and I played her nonstop for several weeks. That's when it all came crashing down.

Facing Fears Alone

Antoinette

I gazed at Jarrett's peaceful, sleeping face as dawn's light slipped across it. My heart felt so full these last few weeks with him that I thought it might burst. I never knew it was possible to be this happy. The sound of him whistling while he flipped pancakes in the little kitchen now as familiar as my own.

Part of me worried I might just be caught up in emotions. I did worry at first we might be rushing things, all lovey-dovey so fast after his last tour left him real battered, inside and out. But I wasn't about to be some cliché army girlfriend, no matter how Mama might disapprove of me settling down. But I knew from the minute Jarrett first walked in that bar that we shared some profound connection.

Now we spent long nights writing lyrics to my melodies, voices mingling in harmony. And even longer learning every inch of each other 'till the bedsheets were tangled chaos. I'd wake flushed to him strumming silly love songs on my guitar. I'd never had that with other men - not feeling so nurtured and free. Like I could leap right off any cliff, wings spread, glorious and soaring.

It wasn't just me feeling more at ease either. Jarrett seemed less tense, too, with those combat nightmares fading somewhat. He said my singing was better at chasing off demons than any military shrink ever was. I think he finally believed there could be a future beyond fatigue watch, burning sands and brothers lost. One with picket fences even, if I dared dream it.

But reality always encroaches, I know that as well as any struggling musician working dive bars dreaming of the big time.

That knock came on Jarrett's door a couple mornings later. Sergeant stern-face delivering marching orders like the Reaper himself. I watched my brave soldier's mask slip into place where my gentle man used to grin back over his black coffee.

The next weeks went by faster than ever. Staying busier than both our jobs allowed trying to pretend deployment wasn't crashing down. All of this brought back memories of my Daddy shipping off when I was no more than seven. I swore no man would abandon me that way twice. Maybe I just traded one lonely life for some hollow lonely nights.

We made love desperate those last nights, like we could fuse together inseparable if we tried hard enough. I clung tight, as far as my nails might dig in, cursing fate and cheap politicians and wars older than my Songbook. If love alone might shield him, I'd have woven armor ten feet thick. But evil exists and they won't never find peace. Duty calls on good men like Jarrett to stand sentry between it and backyard barbeques.

Morning came too soon, cold light, the same as the block of ice that settled in my belly, watching him dress one last time. I made some silly joke about how fine his rear looked, just wanting to picture his smile again. But the laugh choked halfway up my throat so I turned away not wanting him to break down too. We both had to be strong as oak now for what was coming.

Jarrett was packing and instead of helping him like I'd said I would, I'd seduced him with my naked body and was now going to make him late. It wasn't what I meant to happen, but I didn't regret it either. Now, I had to let him go, though it did feel like there was a chance that I was never going to see him again. I couldn't help thinking that this was going to be the worst part of falling for Jarrett, which I had done completely. I was going to have to get used to goodbyes. I wasn't very good at it currently.

"Well, I am going to get out of here and let you finish up. I don't want you to be late because of me."

He chuckled, "Yes you do."

I nodded, "You know that I want you to stay, but this is your job, I get it."

At the airfield, I rushed into his arms with something like a quiet scream building in me. Tears flowed but I kept most wailing locked up in my heart. Just whispering over engines roar my hope - no, my bone deep prayer - that he makes it home once more to me. Because both of us broken birds finally found the missing wings in each other. And this stubborn gal thinks she might not survive losing that sanctuary again.

I kissed Jarrett with even more hunger than our first night, seeking to seal some piece of his warrior spirit tightly within me. I silently swore to wait faithfully no matter how long battles raged half a world away - that shield of love keeping a glimmer of hope alive. I wish that you didn't have to go." I could hear the whine in my voice, and I cleared my throat. "I am going to miss you."

Jarrett pulled me towards him, kissing my lips ever so gently and assuring me that he was going to be back before

I knew it. I didn't believe him. He was going on a mission to Afghanistan and that was all he was going to tell me. Apparently, he wasn't even supposed to tell me that, but I'd overheard him talking in another language and I'd wanted to know what was going on. Now that I knew, it was no better. I actually felt worse if I was completely honest. He was going into a very dangerous situation, something Jarrett did often, and I was supposed to wait around for him to come back. If he came back.

"You know that it's all going to be fine. I do this for a living."

"That doesn't mean that I have to like it. We just found each other and now you're leaving. It feels like I'm never going to see you again." I stopped that line of thinking, simply so I didn't put bad thoughts in the back of his head. He needed to pay attention to what he was doing, far more than I needed to voice my concerns. "I am just going to miss you."

He held me for a time, helping my body to relax, even if he didn't have the words to help my racing mind. "I will be back before you know it."

"I know," I wanted to go into it further, but I might start crying and I didn't want him to remember me like that while he was gone. He didn't know how long he would be, but he promised to get back to me as soon as he can. I needed to hear that and hoped that he meant it. A day without Jarrett was going to feel like too long.

As the transport roared skywards carrying him towards dark unknowns, all I could do was hold on to those last words and keep them close in my heart. I slowly made my way back to my apartment, limbs heavy with emptiness echoing his sudden absence.

***

I'd been filling out my schedule for the week ahead and had accidentally skipped over a routine entry - "visit from Aunt Flo". Glancing back, I suddenly realized I was a couple weeks late on my cycle arriving. My heart began crashing like cymbals echoing loud in an empty club. I couldn't be...could I?

Sitting there stunned, my memories flashed back to our blissful intimate nights together. We often got carried away in the throes of passion, throwing caution aside during those few wonderful weeks. Had we been so completely absorbed in each other in those tender moments that we didn't even think about protection? I thought our love was so new and innocent then. But now a new life is blossoming out of that union. One I don't know if Jarrett is ready to nurture. My heart swells, yet at the same time sinks wondering how this fighter on the front lines will receive such life-altering news.

There was a sinking sensation in my stomach that was hard to ignore. How would Jarrett take this? Would he be happy? Was I happy? There were many questions that had no answer. We hadn't talked enough I realized now. It was usually only a few tidbits while we were recovering, just before we started again. I don't know if that style of conversation was very conducive to learning about one another.

When I found out, I went to go tell Ashley about it. She was my best friend, had been since we'd met in second grade, and I knew that she would at least tell me how she really felt.

I hoped that she would know how I was supposed to feel too, because at the moment, I just felt numb.

***

I knocked and heard Ashley tell me to come in. She was currently braiding the hair of a client and I asked her if she wanted me to come back later. I knew the answer, but it seemed polite to make sure before I plopped down next to her on the burnt orange couch.

Ashley's own hair was braided into tiny little braids that were thin enough to look like hair pieces. "No, Linda here would love to hear some good gossip. I have a feeling that you are about to give me the goods." Linda was older and eager, her black eyes dancing.

"It depends on how you look at it. I don't know if it is good gossip."

"What's it about?" I could see that I had her attention, even if her dark hands kept moving at a rhythmic pace. When I didn't answer right away, her dark, almond-shaped eyes beseeched me.

"It is about a guy." A huge grin spread across Ashley's and her client's face. They both made a nod to tell me to keep going. They were always ready to hear about a love story. We were all hopeless romantics it seemed.

"I am not going to lie, I've been wondering what you've been up to. I should have known that you had found a man."

I sighed and sat back on the couch next to Ashley. She hadn't even got up when I knocked, just hollered to come in. She knew it was me somehow. Ashley always knew. I watched her hands moved swiftly and I was always amazed at how quickly she could finish a braid and be onto the next.

"So, let's hear it. Don't keep us waiting, right Linda?"

The older woman that was getting her hair done nodded and I had both sets of eyes looking at me, waiting for the story that was bound to be good. So, I told them a bit about Jarrett, our meeting and the few weeks that we'd spent in the bedroom after that. I knew that I wasn't going to say anything to make the two women blush, but they certainly leaned forward during the retelling and I couldn't help how nervous I was. I was afraid that they weren't going to see Jarrett in the same way that I did.

Ashley was the first to clarify something, "You went home with him from the bar a couple hours after you met?"

I sighed and agreed, "Well, I mean, Molly's is more of a café than a bar."

Ashley scoffed, "Really, that's your defense?"

She was right, I didn't have a defense. I met a guy that I was attracted to enough to make me forget how things were supposed to work. He'd smiled at me and made me melt where I stood. I didn't know how to explain that to anyone, but soon Ashley would meet him, and she would know exactly what I was talking about. Jarrett was a dream.

The two women didn't cut me any slack when it came time to talk about the real reason I was there. That made everything a bit more intense, and Ashley wasn't joking around anymore. "Are you telling me that you're pregnant? Didn't you guys use protection?"

It was an obvious question, with an obvious answer. We hadn't used it enough apparently.

Ashley agreed, "That's why this is so crazy. This is so unlike you. Jarrett must be quite a man."

I was quick to say that he was, and I felt my face heating up when the two women laughed with my response. He really was something else and I was very much into how he made me feel.

***

Another few weeks went by and the perfect man that I was dying to see, never showed up. I was starting to think that he was not going to come back. I remember the feeling that I had the day we'd said goodbye. I'd felt like I was never going to see him again, though I hadn't imagined that it would be because he'd ghosted me.

After a month of Jarrett being gone, I had to assume that he wasn't going to come back. I'd tried to get in touch with him, calling his phone every one of those days, but I had to stop. I knew deep down that he wasn't coming back. I don't know how I knew, but I did. He was gone.

The worst part of it all was our child was going to grow up without a father. It was the same thing that had happened to me, I never wanted this for my own kids. Would Jarrett ever come back to know that we had a kid? The answer was 'no' in my head, for one reason or another. I was so sure of it that, I was already feeling the consequences of the loss. We'd only known each other a few weeks, but there had been more hope wrapped up into Jarrett, than I'd ever put in anyone before.

I was heartbroken and my hormones were all over the place, making it a normal night time routine to cry myself to sleep. I couldn't see a way out of this. I was going to have a baby soon, alone and I wasn't overwhelmed with good feelings. I missed Jarrett, wanted to know what had happened to him, but knew that I was going to get nothing. Whatever had happened to Jarrett was enough to make him break a promise and I don't think that Jarrett was the sort of man to do that without pause. Which meant something even worse, he couldn't come back.

The last thought should have comforted me, but it didn't. It all just made me sad.

Brought Back from the Brink

Jarrett

When we got the emergency call about the attack on Senator Willis' convoy, my gut twisted into knots. The mission briefing was short on details, but our orders came straight from the top: get in, find the senator, and extract him immediately.

I cursed under my breath as our chopper raced towards the last known coordinates. Willis was chairman of the Senate Foreign Relations Committee, and apparently he'd insisted on some ridiculous photo-op near the Pakistan border despite security concerns. Trying to score cheap political points in the middle of Taliban country — what did he expect was going to happen? If they got their hands on a US senator, it'd be a major strategic and publicity win for them.

As we approached under night vision, the devastation came into focus: smoldering vehicles strewn along the dusty road, dead camels and soldiers tangled together. We inserted a couple klicks away and advanced on foot to the ambush site. Had to be at least a hundred Taliban militants lying in wait — this was no random hit.

We reached the ditch where Willis had supposedly taken cover, but there was no sign of the senator. Just the lingering smell of gunpowder smoke and burnt rubber. I scanned the area through my night vision goggles - some signs of disturbance in the dirt, a few blood spatters maybe. But no body at least. Stanley gestured that he'd found tracks leading away, a group of men by the looks of it. The senator could still be alive if we moved quick.

We followed the trail at a steady clip, senses on high alert for ambushes. Miles of jagged rocks and sparse vegetation blended together in the eerie green glow of our optics. No chatter on comms except occasional check-ins with HQ. Everyone hyper focused. Follow the tracks, get the senator. Avoid detection if humanly possible. Easier said than done with Taliban crawling all over their backyard.

After fifteen klicks or so the landscape changed, more trees and places for cover. Visibility dropped substantially. Hairs on my neck stood up. This would be a perfect spot for them to lie in wait if they realized they were being tailed. I raised my fist to signal a halt. Stanley sank to one knee, scanning right while Ramirez watched our six.

Then all hell broke loose. Crack and thunder of automatic gunfire. Dirt exploding everywhere around us. Ramirez screamed and hit the deck clutching his leg. Stanley dove left and returned fire at muzzle flashes in the tree line. I dropped prone, sighted the first target I could find and squeezed twice. Caught him in the neck right above his chest rig. He swayed like a drunk before crumpling to the ground.

"Sandman Two, this is Epsilon One!" I shouted into comms over the rattle of bullets tearing through foliage. "Under attack, multiple shooters! Request immediate evac, copy?" Static hiss was my only reply. Comms were down or being jammed. Stanley lobbed a smoke grenade then pulled Ramirez behind a boulder to patch him up. Meanwhile I slithered snake-like behind a nearby tree and swapped mags.

We had to rally and break contact if we were getting out of this mess.

For a minute we volleyed fire back and forth looking for any shots of opportunity. Most of the Taliban rebels remained hidden from view. Stanley was trying to lay down suppressing gunfire so I could maneuver to their flank when suddenly my vision went white. A Concussion Grenade landed a few feet away. Rang my damn bell but good for a minute. I blinked blood out of my eyes and tried to shuffle back when strong arms grabbed me from behind.

"Silence, infidel!" growled a voice. Before I could even struggle something slammed the back of my head and everything faded to black...

———

Eyes snapping open to blinding light. Searing pain and loud ringing as my vision slowly came into focus. Sturdy ropes bound my hands behind a wooden chair. An array of tools and implements I didn't want to think much about on the table nearby, stained dark red in places. Two Taliban goons stood glaring with rifles on me while a third leaned against the stone wall sharpening an already gleaming knife. None too pleased with my guest accommodations.

The door clanged open. A new figure strode confidently into the makeshift cell, jet black beard contrasting against his off-white turban. His steady but scornful gaze looked me over like a farmer assessing cattle before slaughter. He barked something in Pashto at the others then pulled up a stool, sat uncomfortably close and studied me silently. This was the head honcho for certain.

"I already know much of why you have come," he stated calmly in accented English. "The man you seek is now beyond your reach. His life will serve a greater purpose."

He let that sink in a moment before continuing. "But you - Jarrett, is it? - may yet be spared if you cooperate fully. There are many secrets still within your head of value." He gestured to the grisly implements on the table. "I trust I need not explain what happens if I deem you to be uncooperative..."

The frigid water splashed my face for the third time, shocking me from my delirium. Through crusted eyes I made out the scowling faces of my captors circled around me. Taliban fighters. I shuddered, only half from the icy chill.

"I ask again, American, what was your mission objective? Who sent you?" barked the interrogator, his glare burning under a black turban.

"Your silence will not save you!" An open hand cracked across my swollen cheek and my vision doubled. Our tenuous rules of engagement hardly applied here now. I clenched my teeth, drawing on every last reserve. A Green Beret did his duty, no matter the cost. Surely my brothers now marshalled assets in the skies above, just as the death of Senator Willis marshalled political fury back on the Hill over my predicament. I had to endure but a little longer before I would be rescued. For now, resistance was my last duty. I steeled myself for the torment.

The attackers that were the bane of my existence in the beginning, came less and less often. I felt like they too had forgotten about me. I was moved from one underground cell to another. I never really knew where I was, but I knew that I was underground, and I was likely never going to be found.

After months, I only asked for death. I tried to stop eating and drinking, but once I was held down and water was forced down my throat, I knew that I was not going to get the easy way out. Instead, I was going to have to live longer in this pain and filth that was my new life.

Imar, my main interrogator, didn't seem to mind that I'd lost all hope in life. He chuckled and made fun of me when he came down. I was no longer the man I used to be. I used to intimidate people, but now I wasn't very intimidating at all. I was a mere whisp of the man I'd once been. They fed me, but not near enough and I hadn't seen meat as long as I'd been here.

"Why don't you just kill me?" I asked Imar one afternoon. He didn't want to talk to me, waved me off, but I wasn't going to be ignored. "Why feed me and move me from place to place? My government won't even admit that I'm here. There is no way that you are going to get anything from me, so why bother?" It was the real question that I wanted to know the answer to. Why hadn't he tried to kill me yet? Didn't he know that if I ever got a chance, I would slowly kill him and all of his friends? I had a picture of them all in my head and if I ever got out of here, all I was thinking about was payback and how sweet it would be to get it.

"For you, too good. I will wait and let you live underground a little longer. We will make money on you, wait and see."

I didn't believe him. No one was coming for me, and no one was going to pay to get me freed. I knew that whatever he thought was wrong. I was going to die here, and all Imar and his friends were getting out of it was some sick joy that I didn't quite understand. How could I relate to such a thing?

The whole time I was in there, I thought of Antoinette. What would she think of me now? She must believe that I'd abandoned her. What else could she think? She would never know.

Why did that thought hurt me the most?

***

After so much time in a dark cell made of dirt, I started to give up on the idea that I was ever going to be rescued. The United States government likely couldn't even admit that I was here. I knew that they weren't going to negotiate for me to go home. That's not how it worked. Everyone in my unit knew what would happen if we were caught. We'd be tortured, likely killed and no one was coming for us. At first, I thought that possibly they would come. I probably held out that hope for a few months, but by month four, I knew better than to believe such nonsense.

That made me want to run away. I tried to, several times, but I never got further then a couple of people in before I was overtaken, beaten and things would get incredibly worse for weeks afterwards. After the third time and the consequences of it, I gave up on what it would take to get out of here. I was going to die under the dirt in Afghanistan. I was sure of it.

So, when one day I heard explosions, gunshots and then yelling in English, someone even calling out my name, I didn't believe it. I couldn't even fathom that it was really someone here to save me, because it was so far from what I believed to be true. When the very cell door in front of me was opened and my name was repeated, a hand held out for me to grab, I still didn't move forward.

"Come on Jarrett, it's time to go home."

They said my name again and though I didn't recognize the man that was holding his hand out for me, I noticed the uniform. It was one of our military. I was actually saved and then I was finally able to move forward. There was a loud explosion, the whole ceiling of dirt on top of us shook and rained loose dirt on our heads. "Let's get out of here. I think they want to bomb this area."

I nodded, "Good, I hope the whole damn tunnel collapses on them."

The soldier smiled with a cool expression. "I would be thinking revenge too after everything they've done. You've been gone a while. They are never going to believe you are still alive, but your unit never gave up hope."

I liked to hear that fact, but there was part of me that was sure this was all in my head. I had waited for rescue for so long that it didn't seem possible. Why now? How? So many questions were running through my head, but none of them mattered enough at the moment. If this was a dream, I never wanted to wake up.

The earth shook underneath my feet, and it seemed like the gunshots never ended. If this was a dream, it could have been more peaceful. I was walking through hell at the moment. I tried my best to focus on getting to the light I could see at the end of the tunnel. When shots fired whizzed past my head and one bullet actually grazed my cheek, I came awake. This was real. I was really getting out of here and the light at the end of it was real. I started to run, my feet finally working, but I fell to my knees moments later when the sun hit me and blinded me completely. How long had it been since I'd had sun on my face?

The sounds were just as overwhelming as the light was and it took me down to my knees. I heard a familiar voice not too long after my knees hit the ground. "Give him room. Where is the damn medic?!"

I turned to see Nathan, one of the members of my team that got away, standing over me with concern on his face. I asked him if he was real, and he agreed that he was. I was starting to realize that this was really happening. I was really going to get out of here and go back to her. Antoinette was the first thing I thought of when I realized that all of this was really happening, and it wasn't just happening in my head. I said her name lightly and he assured me that I would have all the time in the world to see her soon enough. That wasn't all that I wanted to hear, but it was a start.

"Am I really going home?" I said the words lightly, still unsure what I was supposed to say. Was this really happening? Could it be real?

He promised me that I was. I'd served with Nathan most of my time in the military, so it was surreal that he was the one that came for me. I had questions, wanted to know how and why they'd finally come after all this time, but I didn't want to hear the answers. There would be time for that later. Now, I had to worry about all of the things I didn't worry about before. I was in a broken body that before I didn't worry too much about because I wasn't likely to live. Now, I was, and I wanted to get back to Antoinette. I had a long way to go till I was back to the man she met.

"What is the date?" I tried to keep up with the days, but it was impossible when I was moved spot to spot. I lost track at some point.

When I was told the date, I almost fainted. "I've been gone over a year?!"

Ghosts that Linger

Antoinette

The first week without Jarrett I tried to keep busy - working double shifts at the bar, meeting up with old friends, binging Netflix every night to avoid the empty side of the bed. But his lingering scent on the sheets haunted me.

Soon the initial shock faded to a dull gloom I couldn't shake on rainy mornings. My usual vocal warm up scales would catch ragged in my throat as I'd glance through the window mist and still find the gravel drive bare. The promised letters slowed after the first few rushed notes were received. I knew operations overseas made correspondence spotty at best. Still, treacherous doubts crept into my thoughts, leaving me scared and confused.

I stopped working as much as soon as the queasiness and cravings began roiling something fierce - afternoons spent hovering by the bathroom at the bar rather than chatting up customers like usual. I'd stare anxiously at each delivery truck that rumbled past our sleepy block - half expecting Jarrett to bound out the back pulling one of his cockeyed pranks.

By week three the symptoms made denial impossible - I pored over online projections of our child now growing within me. Bittersweet smiles coming easier imagining Jarrett's stunned face nuzzling my soon-to-be rounding belly.

Jimmy kept asking me for a date, suspicion narrowing his gaze at the untouched whiskies he slid over with distracting small talk. But far as townsfolk knew I just caught a lingering flu strain that kept me muzzy for days. Only Mama got the truth over tearful phone calls - how her prodigal daughter somehow found fairy tale love and despair all jumbled in the span of a whirlwind spring. She tutted about consequences but promised to be here when the baby came. I couldn't bear this alone.

By the end of the month, even Mr. Riley at the corner store remarked I looked under the weather. I brushed it off as late nights worrying after reading casualty reports in the paper's back pages religiously. I walked home under the fall leaves that covered the sidewalks in bright orange and red. It made me think sadly of the war happening far away across the ocean that Jarrett was in the middle of.

I rubbed my belly, feeling like it was starting to swell just a little under my loose shirts. But I knew it was much too soon to feel it. Our tiny baby was growing safe inside me - an innocent new life amongst all the violence Jarrett saw every day. I kept praying over and over he'd make it home soon to meet the child he didn't even know about yet. This little miracle brought me hope - proof that beauty and creation can still flourish. I just had to believe we'd one day be a family no enemy could tear apart.

As the waning moon rose outside my bedroom window, I settled in with Jarrett's worn flannel shirt wrapped close inhaling fading traces of his sandalwood aftershave. The last letter I clutched promised he was staying safe - though what tumult raged around him went unspoken between each "I love and miss you, Songbird.

I whispered tearfully to the empty room how his unborn child needed a father, not just a memory preserved under museum glass. Somber visions scored by news reports of another bombing overseas threatened to drown my fragile optimism.

When I saw Nathan coming into Molly's, I knew that it wasn't going to be anything good that he was going to tell me. Nathan was one of Jarrett's best friends in the service. He had this sad look on his face, like he had to tell me something that I would never want to hear. He was surely the bearer of bad news, and I could tell that it was coming for me.

"Hey Nathan. How have you been?" There had been a moment where I looked behind him to see if Jarrett was there, but then I'd seen his expression and knew that there was no one else coming in.

I stopped playing the piano, my fingers still on the keys. I didn't say anything to him, he just stared at me for several moments. He was working up the courage so that he could just say it. Why did I already know what was going to happen? Why could I hear it in my head?

I was stumped as to why he kept staring at me. I had to finally encourage him to say what he came to say, the anticipation was driving me wild. "You can just say it, Nathan."

Here I was thinking that it was going to be bad news. I didn't realize that it was going to be devastating news that was going to change everything.

"He was taken hostage, Antoinette. It's been a while now, we can't find him, but we found who he was with when he was taken, dead. It's only a matter of time..."

I immediately started to cry, the world got dizzy and standing up was literally too much at the moment. "Do you know he is dead?" He made it seem like it was certain.

"We will never know for sure until we find the body," he stopped when I made a pained sound. What was he talking about? A body? When had Jarrett, this vibrant man that I was head over heels in love with, when did he get reduced down to a body? I couldn't handle that fact and I would have done anything to make it different.

Nathan put his arm over my shoulders and then hugged me. I needed it. I thanked him for telling me and he awkwardly mentioned that he didn't want me thinking that Jarrett didn't want to come back to me. "He talked about you every day before the mission."

That was nice to know. I just nodded, unable to speak for the longest time. I almost told Nathan about the baby and how I was carrying his child, but what would be the point? I needed to hold it all in. No one would ever know.

Nathan left and I collapsed. I didn't know how to act now. I'd waited for Jarrett to come back to me, sure that eventually he would. Knowing that he was never coming, was more than I could manage. Without hope, there was nothing left in my hollow heart but pain and regret.

***

The day I found out about Jarrett was the same day that I knew my child was going to have the same father figure that I had, which was none at all. This was never the way I wanted to do things of course and sadly, I didn't know how to fix it. Was I really meant to relive the exact same thing through my child? It seemed unfair and more than a little bit cruel.

It was also the day that I started to look at Jimmy and his passes a little differently. He knew what happened, overheard part of what Nathan had told me and I'm pretty sure he knew that I was pregnant. When he did find out for certain, Jimmy put an idea in my head that I never would have even fathomed before. He knew it all. I was pregnant, and the father was dead, so he offered to give me and my unborn child the one thing that I thought was the most important. He promised to make us a family and though I didn't love him, he was convinced that I would grow to do so. I don't know if that was true or not, but he did make a decent point. It took me a while to come around to his way of thinking, but once I did, I agreed to his terms. I didn't think I would grow to love him and while I wanted to make it clear, it seemed unnecessarily harsh to reiterate such a thing. There was no way to say it kindly.

So about five months along in my pregnancy, I got married to Jimmy and at first it wasn't too bad. He didn't try anything, didn't even expect love, but just the circumstances left me absolutely confused.

I missed Jarrett, stayed up thinking about him most nights. I felt like I betrayed him getting married, even though I reminded myself regularly that it's not like I had a choice to be with Jarrett. I would have chosen to be with Jarrett, would have done anything to make that possible, but I had to accept that sometimes I didn't have control over what happened. As much as I wanted to be happy in this pretend marriage and life that I created, it was impossible not to think about what I'd lost.

***

My son with Jarrett was born a few days early, like he was eager to get started. The love that I had for Jarrett was the most I had ever experienced before, until I met our son, Atticus. Then I finally realized what true love was. It hit me like a ton of bricks and while it was separate from Jarrett, I knew that watching him grow up was going to remind me every day of Jarrett because they had the same eyes and my little bundle of wrinkles was already making expressions that I swear brought Jarrett back into my life again.

I don't know how to explain it, even though it wasn't Jarrett coming back to me, I knew that it was probably as good as it was ever going to get. I also knew that he didn't deserve to grow up without a father so the decision that I had made with Jimmy was the best decision I could have made. Jarrett was gone, but I had a small piece of him to carry with me forever. That was more than I could have ever hoped for.

Jimmy was a really good dad. He was constantly worried about Atticus during my pregnancy and once he was born, he was more attentive than ever before. I loved watching the two of them and for a few days I was content in life and in the decisions that had been made. I wasn't particularly happy with how it all worked out, but I was learning to live with it.

Fate, I was coming to find out was a cruel bitch and even though I hoped with all my might that my sacrifice and decision would bring about something better, that wasn't what happened at all. Instead, I lost everything again in the blink of an eye and the decision that I thought was the best I could make, was reduced to another mistake that I'd made. I thought that marrying Jimmy would give Atticus a father, but instead it just determined his fate in a negative way. Only a few days after

Atticus was born, not even a week to be exact, Jimmy was in a freak accident that took his life.

Part of me wished that he had never proposed to me, and I'd never agree to it. Then he would possibly still be alive. This was all my fault somehow. I felt like the kiss of death, and I knew as impossible as it was, I was just going to have to be both parents for my son and hope that I was able to do a good enough job. I wouldn't dare bring in anyone else into my son's life, simply for the fact that I would worry that something would happen to them. While I knew that Jimmy's death wasn't my fault, it certainly felt like some kind of curse and just to be safe, I decided to back off from that part of my life. As I stood over Jimmy's grave holding Atticus, I made a promise to myself that I would never do it again.

***

This sent me on a trajectory of fierce independence, which was helped dramatically with the fact that as Jimmy's wife, I got everything after his death. It wasn't something that I wanted of course, none of this was, but one of Jimmy's last acts was to give me peace of mind that I never had before with an insurance policy. It gave me time that was sorely needed.

I spent all of my time taking care of Atticus. I didn't work or feel that I could sing for quite a while. I wondered if I would ever have it in me again. I was so filled with sadness. I thought a lot about Jimmy. I missed Jarrett terribly, but with a son that really did look exactly like him, I was comforted with the idea that Jarrett was still with me in some small way. Jimmy haunted me as well, but I had to push them both aside. Atticus kept me waking up, kept me from the deepest steps of depression. He gave me something to live for and after several months, I was able to get back to my life, though I did change a few things. I couldn't work at Molly's again, there were too many memories there. So, I found a new job, somewhere to let off some of the pain and sorrow that I was feeling through my fingers and music.

One day, I had this strange feeling that someone was watching me through the large glass window in front of the Black Cat, where I was working, playing the piano and singing. When I turned and looked nobody was there. For the longest time, I had this feeling that it was Jarrett, and he was back. It made no sense obviously, but it was such a strong thought. It was such a compelling feeling that it made me think it was real.

It was also about that time that Atticus started crying and I had to pick him up to soothe him. He came with me everywhere, including work and me playing music usually calmed him down. This time, it was like he knew something was off.

The rest of the night, I waited with this strange anticipation like something big was going to happen, but it never did. I had to push off the feeling at some point, and the coincidence that I'd been playing 'our' song. I tried to be real with myself, the chances of our song being played was high, because I played it with every set.

When I went home that night, the feeling was gone, and I swear it was like losing Jarrett all over again. I don't know what had me thinking about him so much, maybe it was a certain look from Atticus, I don't know. Whatever it was, it was gone, and I was back to feeling that hollowness in my soul where he used to be.

Lost and Found

Jarrett

Just because I was rescued, didn't mean that I was saved. After almost a year of isolation, poor living conditions and literal torture, I had even more coming for me apparently. I couldn't believe it, but there wasn't much I could do. The military took one look at me and sent me to physical rehabilitation. I had lost considerable weight and muscle mass. I didn't recognize myself when I looked in the mirror for the first time in a year.

As soon as I was rescued, I tried to call Antoinette. Her phone number was no longer in service, so there was no way to talk to her. After seeing myself in the mirror, there was my ego fighting the chance for the two of us to meet. I didn't want her to see me like this. I looked nothing like the man that she knew and cared for. I wanted to get back to that man, so I could get the same feeling out of Antoinette as I had before. I missed her and she was the only reason I made it out of captivity alive, as well as the main muse needed to get me through rehabilitation. I had to do it overseas for the first few months, before I was even fit to fly home.

When I got back Stateside, naturally I wanted to track Antoinette down, but muscle and weight were coming on slow, and I had night terrors to contend with as well. I was quickly given a diagnosis that left me with a medical discharge from the military and then I really didn't know what to do. The Army decided that I was too broken to be of any service to the country and it left me wondering what else was there to do. I hadn't thought of a career outside of the military before.

The new changes didn't make anything easier. It gave me one less thing to look forward to, though to be fair, I don't know if I was capable of going on another mission, knowing that it could end in the same way. Whether it was a good thing or a bad thing, I was no longer going to risk my life for the cause. I had to find a new cause to keep me going and my fall back was Antoinette. I had idolized her and put her on a pedestal in my mind, through captivity and recovery. I just hoped that it all held up to my image of her. I still hadn't been able to get ahold of her. Once I was fit and my rehabilitation was over, once I looked like myself again, I was going to go find Antoinette and make this all right.

That goal kept me going and soon it was time to leave the military structure for good. The VA had been good to me, and I was looking better, if not completely healed. I felt a lot better, but my mind was still plagued with dreams and my body was covered in scars. Through it all though, I was thinking of only one thing. The only thing I was thinking of was getting back to Antoinette and having her back in my arms. Nothing short of that would be enough.

I had to first work on getting my affairs in order. I had been gone for over a year because I was underground in Afghanistan somewhere, and then there was another several months that was needed to get back to some semblance of myself again. Basically, that meant that I had been gone for almost a year and a half. And Antoinette without a clue that I was still alive. Things happened while I was gone. For one, everybody thought I was dead, and they sold my house. Not just that, my truck was gone and the small nest egg that I have been working on was apparently forwarded to my brother. I could live with all of that, but it just made everything more complicated because I had to set up all new accounts which took more time. It took another week or two just to get a driver's license so that I could legally drive around.

When I was finally able to get around and was looking more like my old self, my thoughts turned again to Antoinette. I just needed to find Antoinette, wherever she was. I knew it had been a long time and I knew that the chances of her even wanting to see me after all this time was slim to none, but I still had to do it. I had made a promise to her, and it was one that I had meant to keep.

I'd played out our meeting after all this time a million ways in my head, but I had no real idea of how it was going to turn out. I wanted to believe that everything would turn out fine, but that was likely not possible. How could this turn out alright after everything that had happened? It just didn't seem within reach.

Antoinette was not where I had left her. She no longer lived in the same place, and she no longer worked at Molly's. She had changed her phone number, which wasn't a good sign. I should have known right then and there with that information what I was going to find wasn't going to be good. There was a reason that Antoinette hadn't called me after all this time. There was a reason she had moved and changed her phone. From what I remember, Antoinette had loved her little studio apartment that she lived in, so why would she leave it? Something didn't make sense.

I looked for Antoinette for over a week. I went to all the places I knew that she went to, asked her old boss if she knew where she was and even walked aimlessly in the city where we'd met. It wasn't my finest hour, but I put in the work to find her. I needed to find Antoinette, it was the one thing real in my life and I'd been looking forward to it for so long.

When I didn't find her after many days, it felt like I wasn't meant to. Worse yet, maybe she didn't want to be found and that felt worse.

I was about to give up. Since Antoinette wasn't here and life was too strange now in Kenner without her, I decided that I was going to leave New Orleans altogether. It wasn't the sort of place that I wanted to live anymore, crime was up and most of the friends I had here were gone, and my family was in Wyoming.

There was nothing here for me anymore. Truth was, I tried to figure out what came next. Antoinette was the only person I thought about, and she was the deciding factor. I came here for her, she was the only mission and without her, this place held too many ghosts. We were only together for a few weeks, but they had been jam-packed with checking out the city where we'd fallen in love. It had been love, right?

Walking helped to clear my head, as well as helped me to search for Antoinette. I told myself that fate had brought us together, so if it was meant to be, if I was meant to see her, then she would cross my path. It was putting a lot of faith in something that couldn't be seen or touched, but it was all I had left.

It was the last night that I was going to be here. Kenner had been my home for many years, a place to go to in the midst of chaos, but it held nothing for me now. There were thousands of people, but it felt empty and desolate. I was about to turn around and walk back to the hotel I was staying in so that I could pack up and leave this place, when I heard a familiar melody. It was one that I hadn't heard out loud in a very long time, but it lived rent-free in my head, playing on repeat.

I stopped in my tracks, sure that I was making it up, willing it so much that I was hearing things. I didn't expect it to be real. Someone was playing our song in the Black Cat. The establishment looked a bit lower class than Molly's, but I had hope leap into my chest for the first time since I came back. Could it be her?

There was a large window to see into the darkened interior. I searched to see where the sound was coming from, afraid that it would be a radio or something like that. My whole body relaxed when I saw the familiar black hair and the curved back of the woman I'd been searching for. I didn't need her to turn around as I had before, I knew exactly what Antoinette looked like. I saw her in my dreams every night. I'd found her, fate had brought me right to her. I couldn't believe it!

***

I watched her for a while, playing the song that was ours and feeling all of the same emotions that I'd felt the first time I met her. The desire was there immediately. It had been so long. Too long? I wouldn't know what to do first, but there was a myriad of choices that ran through me, each one better than the last.

I don't know why I didn't move forward. Something stopped me from moving my feet. I don't know what it was, but I couldn't force myself to move. I just stood there for the longest time staring through the window. Why didn't I go in? She was right there, the woman I had been looking for, for longer than I cared to admit. She was all I had thought about while I was underground in Afghanistan. Antoinette was the whole reason I came back to this life at all. I honestly believe that if she hadn't been a memory in the back of my mind, something to go home to, I wouldn't have made it through the punishment of being in captivity for so long. I had heard more than once from a doctor and people in the military who had lived through something similar, that it was a miracle that I'd lived at all. I was called a miracle, but it didn't feel that way. It was Antoinette that saved the day, not me.

Finally, I was able to move. My feet started to plant themselves one in front of the other, taking me closer to Antoinette. I don't know what was going to happen next, I didn't even want to think about it, but I knew that I had finally found her and that was all that mattered. How long had I been waiting to see her face, hear her voice?

I was almost to the door, when Antoinette bent down and picked something up. That something was a child. She gave it a hug, a kiss and I heard her mouth the words 'Mama loves you'. This was her child, and that information blew my mind so much that my feet stopped moving again. How could I move forward when I didn't know what I was going towards? Where did Antoinette get a baby? Why did Antoinette have a baby? When did she become a mother?

Those questions raced through my head, but I got it. I'd been gone a year and a half. Antoinette had moved on. As much as it hurt me to believe it, that's obviously what had happened. What did I expect, really? Antoinette was gorgeous, young and in her mid-20s, of course she was going to move on. I'd been gone a lifetime. What kind of idiot was I? Here I was thinking that she would wait for me as I had been dying for her, but that was a false narrative the whole time. Why would she wait for me, when we had only been together a few weeks? I made it something bigger in my head than it was. Why did the obvious answer hurt so much?

I backpedaled from the door, someone was coming, and I didn't want Antoinette to look up when the bell on the door rang. After all this time waiting for her, I couldn't move forward. I couldn't go to her, knowing that she hadn't waited for me. Now, I felt like an idiot that had held onto something so tightly and for so long, that I didn't even realize there was nothing in my hands to begin with. I was grasping at straws and now the reality was sinking in.

Walking away was probably one of the hardest things I had ever done but seeing Antoinette happy with someone else and a baby, I don't know if I could do that either. I was definitely done with Kenner. There was nothing here for me now, just pain and memories of a life that I would never have again.

Ghost of a Lost Love

Antoinette

"Thanks for letting me stay here, Ashley."

My friend waved me off. "You didn't look like you were fit for travel last night. Are you sure you are getting sleep, because you passed out really fast last night."

I sighed and got up, yawning and checking on Atticus who was lying next to me. We went to sleep on Ashley's couch after coming for a visit. I didn't stay over at her house that much, but it wasn't unheard of. I hadn't wanted to go home to that empty house last night. I was to a point where I was having trouble again and Ashley asked me what was going on.

I shrugged, "I don't know. I just have been thinking about things a lot more lately. I don't know how I got here; you know? I look around at my life and I wonder how I got to the place I am. It makes no sense, but I don't think there is anything I can do to change it. This is my life now."

Ashley smiled and then nodded to Atticus. "It could be worse."

I agreed with her and of course I wasn't talking about my son. I always wanted kids, but there was never a time when I wanted to be a single parent. I don't think anyone started out that way. It was not something I had thought much about. I tried my best to focus on what was next, but there was no telling what that was going to be.

"Yeah, but you know this wasn't what I wanted to happen. I would have done anything to give him a dad, even married Jimmy so Atty would have a father, but that didn't work."

Ashley had that pity look on her face, but that didn't make me feel better. If anything, it made me feel worse about it all. I wanted to tell her that I didn't regret it, but that went without saying. I didn't have to say things like that to Ashley. She knew me well enough. "You know that I don't know what to say Antoinette. I'm always going to be here for you, no matter what. Just know that you two are not alone. I am here."

It was sweet to hear it and I knew that Ashley meant it. I don't know what good it would do me if I was completely honest, but just hearing that I had someone on my side was likely more than enough. I try not to focus too much on the bad. I needed to focus on the good and Ashley was right. Atticus and I weren't alone in the world, but sometimes it felt like it.

"You've been thinking about Jarrett again, haven't you?"

Sometimes Ashley knew me a bit too well, but I gave her the truth. She was right. I had been thinking about Jarrett a lot more than usual. I told her about the feeling I had the other day. It was so strong and came out of nowhere that it made me really think that maybe he had been close by. I don't know why he wouldn't have stopped and said something to me, but I couldn't help thinking that he was there. I think we both knew that him being there was impossible. He was dead. So, how could I feel like I was losing him again?

Atticus got up not too long after I did, likely all the talking that me and Ashley were doing. I told Ashley that I was going to take off and she reminded me like the great friend that she was, that she was here if I needed anything. Once again, I don't know what I would have done without her. Ashley had been a good friend for years. I know she was sick of hearing me whine about Jarrett, but I couldn't help it sometimes.

Jarrett was the man that made me fall in love with him and then he was gone just as quickly as he came into my life. I don't think I was going to be able to ever feel the same way about anyone else. Anytime someone hit on me at the bar, which happens quite often, I didn't even pretend like I was interested, because I knew that I wasn't. Nothing and no one would ever measure up to him. Jarrett could not be replaced and that might have been the worst of it. It wasn't that I was going to be alone, but that there could be no other way. How could I replace someone that in my eyes was perfect?

***

The next night at the bar, I swear there was something in the air. I had two guys hit on me, and since I was in a weird mood, I didn't say no in the same way that I usually did. They said that they were into me, so I mentioned a baby at home that needed a dad. Not surprisingly, neither one were interested after that. If I thought dating was hard before, I had no inkling of just how hard it could become. Single mothers certainly got a bad rap and widows were in the same boat. I don't think that I wanted to date or anything like that, but maybe it was the idea that it was never going to happen again that bothered me so much. I wasn't that old.

I was sad to realize the futility, but also to give up on Jarrett's love. I would never find anything better, so why try?

He had raised my standards too high, and it couldn't be matched, so in a way he ruined me for any others.

I went home with the realization that this was as good as it was going to get. I had Atticus. I had my music. What more could I ask for? Of course, I wanted to ask for Jarrett. I did dare want more, but I wasn't going to get it. Instead of pushing him out of my mind though, when I got home that evening, I showed Atticus the few pictures I had of his dad. I found it hard to look at the pictures, but then again, my son looked just like him, so it's not like I could ever get away from it. Atticus did have his own, unique features, lighter hair, but the eyes were hauntingly the same. I couldn't look at my son and not think of Jarrett.

I went to bed that night with Jarrett on my mind a little bit more than usual. It wasn't the first time that I had gone to bed thinking about him, but it was the first time that I realized I would go to bed with him on my mind for the rest of my life. I'd always thought in my far away thoughts that one day it would change. I don't know what exactly I thought was going to change, but I was starting to understand that nothing was.

There were also dreams that I kept having about Jarrett. Ones where he came back, and they were usually good dreams. Tonight, this time around, bit wasn't a good dream at all. It felt like no matter what I did, he was gone. Jarrett was never coming back. I don't know why but tonight, I finally realized that for good. I woke up drenched in sweat and truly feeling distress. Why was I sobbing?

***

Ashley called me in the morning to find out if I was doing alright. I don't know what I had done to get blessed with such a good friend, but I assured her that everything was going to be fine. It wasn't, I shook as I held the phone, but how could I even explain this anyways, even to her?

"You were a little bit off the other day when you were over here. I just wanted to make sure that you're alright. I've been working and I didn't get to call you last night like I wanted to."

Ashley worked as a bartender, and she had ridiculous hours like me. I told her that she didn't have to worry about me and that I was going to be fine. I hoped it was true, didn't know if it was or not. After over a year and a half, I would think that I wouldn't dream about him every single night anymore, but it was actually getting worse. It made no sense, why was Jarrett back on my mind again?

"It is crazy to think that he could come back, right?" I said the words. I couldn't stop.

Ashley was quiet for a moment. "You don't really think he's going to come back, do you?" She asked the question like she was concerned with the answer, like she was concerned with my sanity or something, but I assured her that I didn't think he was going to come back. I hoped he would, but after the 3rd or 4th month, I realized that he likely wasn't going to. I still wished it though.

"No, I don't think he's going to come back, but I don't know, I just feel like something is going to happen. I don't get this feeling very often and I can't shake it. For one reason or another, something tells me that Jarrett is going to be back in my life. I know it sounds crazy, I know what Nathan said and I believe him, even though I didn't find anything when I looked it up. I just have a feeling."

I heard it in my voice, saw it in her eyes. She was looking at me as if I might have lost my mind, and she pitied me, and I think that probably bothered me more than anything. Ashley was the one that knew me the most. I wanted her to take this seriously, because I certainly was. I don't know why, but I could feel it deep in my soul that something big was about to happen. I wanted my best friend to believe it too. I needed someone to believe me, and I desperately wanted it to be Ashley. The silence between us was deafening.

"Well, I'm not going to hold you up, I know you got things to do today." I had to get off the phone with her because there was nothing but bad vibes coming out of the conversation. I was already having an off day. I didn't want to add any more to it.

Ashley said something about how she hoped it was all going to work out, but I knew she didn't mean it. She thought that I'd lost it. I hadn't. Something was up and I could just feel it. Why didn't she believe me? Would I believe her if the tables were turned?

When I hung up with her, I tried to push away the negativity. Ashley was probably right. She was the one that was a lot more levelheaded than I was. I was trying to be but failing miserably. The whole time I was getting ready for the day, I was jittery and waiting for what came next.

Long-Awaited Reunion

Jarrett

"You were wrong."

I'd just walked into Nathan's office, and he shook his head at me. "What are you doing here and what's my fault?" He turned around, adding that I was looking good.

"If I look good now, that must say something about how bad I looked last time you saw me."

Nathan agreed, "You look better, put on some weight. Are you here to tell me that everything is going well for you?"

I scoffed; he should have known better than that. I felt like I was on a one way to hell at this point. All this time I'd spent waiting, hoping, dreaming about the time that Antoinette and I would get back together, it was all spoiled. Nathan was the one that told me I should go find her. He was sure that she would be happy to see me, said she'd been upset when I was MIA.

"So, what was I wrong about?"

"Antoinette."

Nathan sighed, "I thought for sure that she would be happy to see you. What happened?"

"She didn't see me, because I saw enough of her."

Nathan wanted to know what that meant, and I told him what I'd observed when I finally found her, as well as how she had changed her number and address.

"Do you want my knee-jerk reaction?"

I told him that I did. Nathan was a smart man and he had saved me. I trusted him and what he had to say. I braced myself for his words though, I knew I wasn't going to like them.

"She seems like she has moved on. Did you see a ring on her finger?"

I tried to remember, closed my eyes to see the scene again and I could have sworn that she did have a ring on. Why hadn't I remembered that before? Was it because I hadn't wanted to?

"I was afraid of that. I just can't believe she would find someone else."

Nathan sighed, "She is a beautiful woman."

I agreed, I knew that much. I knew that Antoinette was one hell of a catch, but I didn't want to believe that something had happened like that. Could she have moved on? It was what I thought, but I had to be sure. I felt like if I was going to leave Kenner, walk away from the woman keeping me alive all this time, taking up my thoughts and feelings, I should know for sure that there is no way we can be together. If there was any chance, I wanted to work on it. We needed any chance we could get.

"I have to know what happened."

Nathan knew what I was asking right away, which was nice because I didn't think I could say it out loud. It was unlike anything that I'd ever wanted to do before. "I can look into it for you."

I nodded that that's what I wanted, and I was elated. He was the guy on the team that was always looking for all the information. I wanted to not have to do it, but I trusted Nathan to find out the truth and to keep it all to himself if that's what was necessary.

"You look like you need a drink. Why don't you settle in for a bit and let me make some calls?"

I thanked Nathan, knowing that he would find whatever was hidden that I needed to know. Nathan was good at so many things, but he was best at finding information. He had connections because he did the work. I went to his fridge and grabbed a beer. I wouldn't be here long, but beer always helped. I took a sip and waited anxiously. It felt like Nathan was going to find out my fate now and I didn't like my fate to be in anyone else's hands but mine.

***

"You were so worried about it that you took a nap, huh?"

I sat up, groaned at the headache developing. I had just rested my eyes for a minute. "Sorry, I haven't been sleeping well. Hotel beds remind me of the barracks."

"Well, I found out some information on her, but I don't know if you are going to like it or not."

He was preparing me, which wasn't good. That left me wondering how bad it could be, if he was felt the need to warn me first. "Don't be shy, just come out with it."

There was a pause and then Nathan sat down. "You were right, she did move on. She got married a few months after you left, a few weeks after I saw her. She had a baby a few months later, so she must have been with him very quickly after you left."

That hurt, he was right. I wasn't going to like this at all. I'd seen the baby, well toddler, actually, and I saw the ring. Why did I insist on coming all the way over here, just to be told what

I already knew? I don't know what was wrong with me, though now I knew that everything that I feared was valid. Now what?

"Well, thanks for checking it out for me Nathan, I owe you one."

Nathan waved me off and stopped me when I started to sit up. "I think you should keep listening, because I found out more."

I shrugged, "What more is there to talk about? She is married and has a kid. I think that is all the information I need Nathan, don't you?"

He pressed his lips together, "There is more."

Nathan waited for me to nod because I wanted to hear it. I knew there was nothing more that would make any of it better, or at least that was what I thought. As wrong as it sounds, finding out that Antoinette's husband had died not long after they married, leaving her a widow, did just that.

"You're kidding?"

Nathan pushed his fingers through his blonde hair and sighed, "Nope, that's what I found out. She has not had much good luck since you left either."

He was right, I did want to know that, but I didn't know what I was supposed to do with the information. Now what? I tried to consider all my options, but before too long, I was trying to figure out what came next with Antoinette. When I left Nathan's house, I was more confused than ever before, but at least now it was real concerns and not the ones my mind came up with. When it was me coming up with ideas left and right, there was no end to the mental suffering. This way, at least I knew where I stood.

***

That realization led me back to the Black Cat where I had seen Antoinette before. I had thought about it, until I concluded that I had to see her again. I was hurt that she had apparently not even waited long at all before she got with another man and got pregnant, but I hoped that it was something that I would come to understand her side of, and be okay with it. I had to hear what happened, even if it was likely to be a tense conversation, it was one that we had to have.

It took me several minutes to get up the courage to go inside the establishment. I had no idea how this conversation was going to go. Maybe I should wait a little longer. I certainly had a lot of feelings about this and there were no good ones. I wanted answers to questions that weren't likely mine to ask.

I also knew that I was going to have to answer why I hadn't come back when I said I would. That promise had not been realized, but it was not any fault of my own obviously. I wanted to come and see her. I would have given anything to keep my promise. I'd spent so much time thinking about her and the moment that we would see each other again. It was paramount in my mind, and I knew in the back of my head it would never turn out to be as good as I had imagined it to be.

I wanted the fantasy. I wanted her to have waited for me, where she couldn't move on because she didn't know how. I don't know what I expected, but I didn't expect Antoinette to have a baby and get married so soon after I left. Maybe I was here just for that answer more than anything else, because as I watched her playing through the window, those questions of why were all I could think of.

Someone almost hit me with the door as they were leaving, and I was finally able to get my head together. I apologized and then slipped inside, catching the door as they left. It felt like it was now or never, and I cringed a little bit at the sound of the bell jangling on the top of the door. I'd watched her for a while and just like at Molly's, she got so into what she was doing that she would be completely immersed, not seeing anything else.

It was different this time though. She started the first few notes of our song, but she almost immediately stopped playing and turned around. There was this moment when our eyes met, that I don't think I will ever be able to forget. It was like before, this instant connection pulled us together. This time, she stood up immediately and started walking towards me.

She had a tear in her eye by the time she got to me. I don't know what kind of reaction I was looking for, but this wasn't it. There was relief, attraction, love, hope, all of these emotions just written right there on her face. I was feeling just as much if not more and when she stopped just inches from me, the first thing I knew to do was kiss her. It was all I'd dreamed about.

Her lips were soft, and they immediately moved with mine. The connection that I'd felt all this time was even stronger than before. This was what I was looking for. I knew deep down that I'd been waiting for her to be whole again. She was what kept me going and having her back in my arms took away all the pain and suffering that I'd had since the last time we met. If all of that was done for me to get back to her, it was worth it.

An intrusive thought pushed through. I had to wonder if this was all a game to her. How could she come to me with such a hello, but never wait for me at all? My mind was cutting into the moment, but then her body rubbed up against me suggestively, and it was all I needed to forget my worries once again.

She made a sound that cut into me like a knife, and I was no longer able to remember the fact that we were in an establishment that she worked in. If I had been given even a few more seconds, I would have likely tried to set her on a table, so that I could have her at the perfect height. I was already thinking about it, shaking inside with desire because I could almost feel her velvety folds. It's exactly what I needed.

Antoinette pushed me away. For whatever reason, she broke the connection, and I was finally able to breathe. It also meant that I was able to think again, which probably wasn't the best thing when my mind was considerably leaning towards the dark side. Our touch had made me forget for a little while, but now, I wasn't sure how to feel, though my whole body was still trembling from our touch.

"I thought I'd never see you again," the words slipped out before I could stop them.

Antoinette nodded, pressed her lips together and then took a step back. There was something going on internally with her that I didn't quite understand.

"Let me tell Mary that I am done for the night. I have a little while before I must get home. We can have a drink and talk, go for a walk, your choice."

I pointedly looked at the ring on her finger and she kind of chuckled nervously and moved her hand out of my line of sight. This was going to be hard, but having an Antoinette back in my arms was incredible, even better than I had imagined. Could I keep the intrusive thoughts out long enough to have a proper reunion?

Unresolved Tensions Surface

Antoinette

I couldn't believe my eyes when I saw Jarrett standing in front of me. I'd even been told I was crazy by Ashley for thinking of him so hard. I knew that it was crazy for me to think that I'd see him again after all the time we had been apart, but he here was. I couldn't stand how good he looked. I dropped the song playing, our song and I ran towards him. I would later think of the moment as embarrassing, but then we'd shared that perfect kiss, which had me questioning everything.

Like before when we first met and we spent those three and a half weeks together, I'd been unable to get out of his reach. When his hands were on me, I couldn't think of anything but him. All this time later, everything between us and that was still the same. I didn't want it to be so, I felt like he was able to control me in that way and I didn't like the feel of it at all. I wanted something more.

So, I pulled back and put some distance between us. It was the only thing that was going to keep me sane. Jarrett had all the same draw to him, and I was someone that could do nothing but get pulled in. Still, after not seeing him for so long, my insides crumbled with his proximity. I could barely breathe. What was wrong with me?

I took another step back and told him that I was so glad to see him. I wanted to burst out with how I thought he was dead. I'd been told that likelihood of his survival was very low. I didn't want to believe it then, but all that time came and passed. He never came back. Of course, I was going to think the worst.

It also made me immediately realize what I had to tell him. I'd been married, widowed and I became a mother. I wasn't sure how to explain any of it and it all felt problematic. I didn't know how he was going to respond. This was a mine field.

I went to my boss; said I was leaving for the day and took a long walk with Jarrett. I needed to move, or I knew what was going to happen. I was going to fall into those strong and safe arms of his and never want to get out of them. I could live in his arms; I swear I could.

"I thought I'd never see you again, truly Antoinette."

I nodded. I felt the same way. We walked a short distance and I think I was waiting for him to say something. Likely, he was waiting just as well, because he said nothing for the longest time.

"I know what has happened since I've been gone. I had someone find out for me."

He said the words out of the blue and I had no idea what he was talking about. When I asked him, he shrugged, "I just want you to know that I know it all. There doesn't have to be this weirdness between us. Let's just say now, I know what you did."

It was the way he said it that made me really pay attention. It was slightly accusatory, and I thought to myself, if he knew what happened, then how in the world could he judge me? Did he know everything-everything? I wasn't going to play under the likely false assumption that everything to him, meant the same to me.

"You are going to have to tell me what you think I did to you." Just like he hadn't been able to keep the accusation out of his tone, I was just as unable to keep the sound of disappointment and hurt out of mine. I don't know what he thought had happened, what I'd done, but I wasn't going to listen to it. I couldn't. I had done nothing wrong and even when I wasn't sure of the validity of that claim, I still used it. It had always felt like a betrayal to marry Jimmy.

"You had a baby and got married very quickly after I left. It wasn't pleasant to come back and find out that you'd taken to another man so quickly from my departure. I thought we had something special..." Jarrett shrugged and then sighed like he didn't want to say what he was saying. "You know, I just know, okay."

I'd came to a full stop when he had started down this road. I wanted to tell him what had really happened and why all those things were true that he said, but there was another part of me that couldn't believe what he said. He had no idea what he was talking about. Yeah, he knew a little bit about what had happened while he was gone, but it definitely wasn't something that I was going to talk to him about, not like this. I hadn't done anything wrong. I had done what needed to be done and I wasn't going to defend myself to him.

My eyes narrowed and I asked him how he knew all of this about me. He hadn't been around, so how does he know what's been going on?

"I have a friend who looked you up. It's not to upset you or anything."

I was a little flabbergasted by him, because Jarrett knew that he was not being fair. How could he imagine that he was?

He waited for me to what, apologize? I didn't feel like I should have apologized. I got married, and I had a baby while he was gone, that didn't mean what he thought it meant.

"Wow, you coming here like this, and the first thing you have to say to me is about what's happened since you were gone? I don't know how you thought this would turn out well. You have no idea what you're talking about. You may have had somebody look me up, but how would they know anything? You're making a lot of assumptions here don't you think, Jarrett? Especially for someone who pissed off and stayed gone over a year. You told me that you would be back as soon as you could. Where have you been!?"

I might have yelled the last part, and I will be the first to admit that I wasn't happy about how I responded. I never thought I would see him again, but if I had thought it possible, I never would have wanted it to go down the way that it was. This was painful. I was so near tears that I just turned and basically ran away. It wasn't my finest moment and Jarrett didn't come after me. What did he think of me, to ask me such questions?

When I got to my car I was shaking. I wasn't going to go back into work, because I already told them that I was leaving for the day. I wasn't sure what I was going to say to anyone if I went in like this anyways. I was clueless how I had let myself get so worked up. What made me say those things? Was it because I felt the guilt that he was leveling at me? I would have never married if I would have known...

Then, another idea came to me. It wasn't like I had made up the idea of him being dead in my head. I hadn't made assumptions, one of his friends had come to me and told me that he was missing. Nathan said that they didn't think he'd made it and they had stopped looking for him. He had been so genuine; he'd made me believe him and I'd made decisions from that conversation. Was it real or was it all made up? Why had Nathan come and said such things if they weren't true?

I waited for what felt like an eternity for Jarrett to come find me. I ran away, half-expecting him to chase me, but where was he? I looked around and realized after a time that once again, he wasn't coming. Could I blame him? He likely had things he didn't want to tell me, and it wasn't like I was acting all that sane currently. It was hard to act like I didn't care when it was Jarrett. With him, I always cared too much.

Finally, I left the parking spot and looked around for Jarrett as I was leaving, I didn't see him around and while I wondered where he'd gone, I knew that I wasn't going to see him again this night. It was better to get home and see my son. Hope for him having a father surged, but I was going to have to do a better job next time I saw Jarrett. If I was going to see him again.

I worried that I'd messed everything up and that was going to hurt Atticus. He was all that mattered. What I had with his father was a long time ago and apparently it wasn't as perfect as I as I remember it being. Instead, it was complicated and the more I thought about Jarrett, the more I knew I was lost. By the time I got home, I was trembling inside, and I held Atticus longer than ever before. One way or another, I knew that things were about to drastically change. I wasn't sure if I was ready for it or not.

"Are you ready to meet your daddy, Atticus?" I asked my son in a sing-song voice. If only he knew what I was saying. I needed to talk to Ashley. She would know what to do and a part of me wanted to be like, told you so. I knew that Jarrett was coming back, but I didn't know how visceral it was going to be. I didn't realize that seeing Jarrett again was going to make me run to him and cling to him when I saw him. After that it was just downhill.

When I laid down that evening, Jarrett naturally overwhelmed my every thought. I couldn't wait to see him again, knowing that I would, even though today was a trainwreck. Fate wouldn't have brought him back into my life for no reason. I knew for certain one thing, I'd see him again and this next time, I swore that I'd be ready. I even called his number once, willing myself to face Jarrett and say what needed to be said, but I'd chickened out before he answered and hung up. Maybe tomorrow.

Surrendering to Passion

Jarrett

I don't know what happened. One minute I was happy to see Antoinette, we were kissing, she was in my arms and the whole world was where it was supposed to be. Antoinette had been exactly what I needed, and the way she felt was just as amazing as she had been before. It was all so perfect, but then it wasn't.

We'd left, walked and talked. Then I had burst out with what my mind was on. Of course, it was likely the last thing that I was supposed to say. I wasn't supposed to mention what I'd found out, but it had all just tumbled out. Before I could say anything more, I was truly in the depths of despair because Antoinette popped off defensively and ran off. I'd waited so long to see her and in a matter of minutes I'd messed it up and she'd taken off.

Since I figured she would go back to the Black Cat, that's where I sat. I picked a spot at the bar, ordered a drink and waited for Antoinette to calm down and come back. We had a lot to get through and while I had said too much, I was going to make sure that I didn't do it again.

I waited for a lot longer than I originally set out to. I hoped that Antoinette would come back, but she never did. I had a few drinks, tried to get my head around what had happened. I didn't want to tell Antoinette where I'd been, though I knew I was going to have to. Antoinette thought that I'd ran off and just never bothered to come by and see her. That couldn't be any further from the truth. I was stuck and unable to see her. I wanted to, but she didn't know what sort of obstacles were between us. I had to imagine when she did figure it out, she would forgive me, as I was going to have to forgive her. I wanted things to move forward and even though I was hurt with the pregnancy, baby and husband, I would be more hurt if I didn't have her in my arms again. I learned a long time ago to pick my battles, no matter how hard it could be at times.

After deciding that I was just going to have to come at this a different way, I asked the bartender about Antoinette and where she was staying. The woman was blonde and had a great smile, but as soon as I asked about Antoinette, the smile was gone, and she didn't want to give me the information that I wanted.

"Why would you want to know about the singer?"

I felt like this wasn't going to end well. She acted like she was jealous, I could feel her attention, but I had no desire towards her at all. I felt nothing for any other woman since Antoinette and that wasn't going to change.

"We go way back, and I missed her earlier. I want to talk to her, but I don't know where she lives anymore. I've been out of town for a while."

Tiffany scoffed and said that there was no way that information about where she lived could come out. She asked me again if I wanted to go somewhere with her, she didn't seem to care what sort of relationship Antoinette and I had. I was amazed at her brazenness. It didn't make me want her but pity her. I was not going to get what I needed from Tiffany, so I left, telling myself I would be back the next day.

I decided that night I wasn't going to leave Kenner now, not yet. I wanted to know what was going to happen with

Antoinette. I had to know. I'd found her and I wasn't going to let one misunderstanding keep us apart. I was just going to have to figure out what to do next.

***

The next morning a little bit later when the Black Cat opened, I was the first person in the door. Just because the bartender from the night before didn't tell me what I wanted to know, didn't mean that I wouldn't get the information from someone. I was known around, and I was not above using whatever I had to get my way.

This time around I talked to the owner, and I thought I was going to have to give our whole life story and our love story, really pull some heartstrings, that's not at all what had to happen. The owner was male and once I told him that I was just coming from a mission in Afghanistan, I got all the information I could want and then some. He apparently wanted to go into the military when he was younger, but he didn't know if it was right for him. I assured him civilian life was likely the way to go for most.

I started out towards Antoinette. I got the address to her place and while I wasn't completely sure that she was going to be happy to see me in the beginning, I hoped that after a little while she would be. I would do better this time and keep my mouth shut.

I stood in front of her door for the longest time because I was ridiculously nervous. Last time I had mucked it all up and I was afraid of doing that again. I wanted her to understand that I would have been here sooner if I'd been able. I also wanted her to know how much she meant to me, how she had saved me by just being herself. I had so much to tell her, and I would not be able to stop until everything that had happened since I left was out on the table. Then, if she didn't want to be with me, that would be her own choice, but she at least needed to know the truth.

My hands hovered to knock and finally I just did it, knocking hard and waiting for a minute. It was still early, just before noon, but I was hopeful that I would catch her at home, and we would finally be able to have that discussion that we desperately needed to have. I was full of all kinds of thoughts and feelings. I couldn't wait to see what came next.

Antoinette answered and even though I was expecting her, I wasn't expecting my heart to leap into my throat and for my body to have such a strong feeling towards seeing her again. I remembered the kiss that we had shared and naturally I wanted that again.

"Jarrett?! What are you doing here?"

I smiled and hoped the grin conveyed my apologies and desire for amends. "Yesterday didn't go so well and I was hoping that we could have a discussion that didn't end the same way. We never used to have trouble talking before."

Antoinette scoffed, "I don't think that we talked that much before. I bet that's why we didn't have any trouble with it. We were always far too busy doing other things, weren't we?"

I don't know why she was bringing up such things, but I couldn't help feeling the tightening in my pants when she did so. I was shaking from the reminder. Was that her intention?

Antoinette moved back to let me in, and I don't know why, but I could tell that this meeting was going to be different than the last. I was going to come clean with the secrets that I was carrying with me, and I had to hope that she would understand. It was a lot to take on, but I knew that Antoinette was worth it. It was just hard for me to share such personal and painful information.

She shut the door behind me, letting me pass. The first thing I did when I got into the living room was look around and I noticed we were not alone. The baby that I had seen before was not such a tiny baby anymore. I could see that he was maybe even a year old. Nathan hadn't said exactly how old the baby was, just that she had gotten pregnant very quickly after I left. I know that that information bothered me, but I was here for a reason. I wanted to push it all behind us and move forward. I had already decided that being without her wasn't an option. It just meant that I was going to have to find a way to live with the past because I wanted Antoinette for my future. I was willing to do what was necessary, and it all started with a big dose of honesty that neither one of us was going to have too much fun dealing with.

"So, what did you want to talk about Jarrett? I'm not even going to ask how you found me. I guess your source struck again."

I could tell that Antoinette wasn't happy with me. I had some explaining to do and this time I wasn't going to let my mouth override my ass, no matter how easy it was to do. "I wanted to talk to you about why I was gone so long."

Antoinette waved me off, "I was upset and shouldn't have said that. I am sure you had your reasons, but I did wait for you. Nathan came and said that you were MIA."

"I was. I was captured by the enemy and imprisoned for over a year. Nathan is the one that helped bring me back. I promise that I came to you as soon as I could. I had months of rehabilitation and then you were my next stop."

Antoinette gasped with some of my retelling, and I kept it light. Antoinette never needed to know everything, just enough for her to know with assurance that I wasn't staying away because I had a choice. I came back to her as soon as I could, as I promised, though I never thought it would take this long.

Just about the time that I was going to finish my story, her son got fussy, and I watched her feed him and then settle him down for a nap. Only about twenty minutes had passed since I got there, but I was already more relaxed then when I started.

Antoinette came back into the room, and she had an amazing smile on her face. She always looked so beautiful and natural. I wanted to kiss her again, but I knew something more had to happen first. She looked like she already forgave me, which was more than I could have asked for.

When she moved towards me and let me pull her into my arms, the first and most natural thing for me to do was to kiss her. My lips were dying to be on hers since I'd went to see her the day before. My whole body was dying for her. I was rock-hard already without so much as the first kiss down. Antoinette's body settled in against mine, curving its way around me until I couldn't tell where her body ended and mine began. It was hard for me to focus when her limbs slithered around me.

The next thing I know, I have Antoinette picked up and I am starting to ask her where her bedroom is. "We can't go in there. It's right next to Atticus' room and I don't want to wake him up."

"All you have to do is keep the noise down." As soon as I said it, I knew that it would be too much to ask. Antoinette was a very vocal lover and while I loved it more than I could say, I didn't want to wake her baby up. I thought that I could cover her mouth and let her scream out against my hand, but I knew that wouldn't do it either. "Where then?"

Antoinette waved me off and said that I was horrible. I would take that critique, if she pointed me in a direction. When she didn't, I pushed her back against the wall and pressed my hard length up against her. Since her legs were wrapped around me and there was barely anything between us, I could feel her heat and she could feel my rigidity. I heard that telltale gasp that I loved to hear so much. Antoinette wanted more, she was dying for it, and she whimpered in my ear, taking my mind off of everything else. "Please don't make me wait any longer!"

With her words, my mind and hands went into a frenzy. How long had I needed to hear those words? Now that I had heard it said out loud, I wasn't going to waste any time. I needed to be inside of her right now and since she was begging for it, who was I to keep her waiting? It didn't seem right.

Swept Away by Desire

Antoinette

One minute I am begging for him to take me and the next minute, he was. I had a lot to work through when it came to Jarrett, we both did, but that wasn't what I worried about right now. At this moment, all I could think about was how good Jarrett was going to feel inside of me and I had no time at all to imagine it. Jarrett had my bottoms off and my panties pushed to the side in seconds.

"Don't stop, please!"

Jarrett gritted his teeth and then chuckled. "I don't think I could, even if I wanted to."

With his words, he dropped me. I hadn't even known he was holding me up, but as soon as he let me go, I slid down his full length, my wetness giving him every inch in seconds. I called out his name in pleasure. I couldn't believe how great he felt and the sounds coming from my mouth were unstoppable. I shook in his arms, feeling every bit of him. I swear he'd grown since we'd been together.

"You're tighter than I remember."

I scoffed; he didn't need to know that I thought he'd grown. He didn't need to know that the reason I pushed back on his chest was because he was widening my insides with his girth. When Jarrett's lips found mine, he covered up the whimpers that came out of me that I was unable to control.

Jarrett felt amazing and since he had me propped up against the wall, there was nowhere for me to go. I had to

70

take all that he gave to me, even when everything about it was overwhelming. I came so hard in a few minutes, that I didn't think I was going to be able to walk straight again. He nailed me to the wall, pushing deep and gave me no recovery time. This was the man that I remembered well. It was surreal to have him back inside of me, but better than ever. I hadn't been with anyone since Jarrett and now I knew why, there was no comparison. I clung to him and never wanted to let go.

He picked up the pace, my whole body rocking up and down against the wall. It knocked a picture down, but it didn't stop Jarrett, not even for a second. He just moved faster until I exploded underneath him. That finally broke his hard exterior and I could see on his face that his resolve cracked with it.

Jarrett kissed me hard and I felt his need fill me up all the way. I was full of him, his seed and I pushed back against his chest. My legs were shaking, but I knew I had to stand. Jarrett stood next to me, breathing hard and focused on my bare legs. I forgot the butterfly that I'd gotten tattooed after talking to Nathan. Jarrett was now looking at it hard, "What does that say?"

"Nocturne," I said the words quietly because I knew that I was going to have to explain it and I really didn't want to. I was still steamrolled by how I felt with him, and I didn't want to ruin it. He might not understand.

"What does that mean?"

"It's the name of a song."

"Our song?" Jarrett wanted to know immediately.

"Yeah." I could barely say the words, but I am glad I did. He was staring hard when I was able to look up again.

"You never did forget about me, did you?"

I agreed that I hadn't, "How could I Jarrett? You're pretty unforgettable." I nodded to the fact that he was just as hard and needy as he had been earlier. "And you are always ready for more. Been a long time?" I joked because it was something that I had said to him years before.

This time though, a sober look came on his face. "I have waited for you all this time."

He was telling me that he'd been with no one else. I wanted to say the same thing, it was true, but I wasn't given a chance. Jarrett pulled me in and kissed me seconds later. I could barely hold back his desires and I had intention on it.

***

A little later Atticus woke up and I introduced Jarrett to his son. I didn't say the words, I was terrified to, so I wanted the two of them to meet and see how it all went. I worried about Jarrett's reaction, but I had hope if we took it slow. Jarrett wasn't standoffish, but he wasn't comfortable with young kids either. I could see that.

So, we went to the park and did some fun things that would keep the good feeling going. There was a lot that had to be talked about, so much that I had to tell him about, but for this one moment in time, I could look at father and son playing together and dream that it would always be like this.

"He's a cute kid."

I agreed. I wanted to say something about how he looked just like his father, but that wouldn't end well. I couldn't believe that the words even came to me like that, but there was nothing else that I could do. I wasn't good with keeping secrets and by the end of the day, Atticus asleep for the night, I was ready to spill it all. Jarrett had other thoughts though and I couldn't stop his will. I quickly didn't want to.

Jarrett moved the dishes off the table and I told him not to worry about the dishes. I would get them later. I was nervous about what I was about to tell him. Jarrett didn't notice or took it a different way, because the next thing I knew, he was sitting down next to me, and his hand was gently on my cheek. I asked him what he was doing, and he said something about admiring me. "I have to keep coming over here and touching you. I can't believe that you're really here. I have waited so long..." His voice trailed off and I could see his eyes were somewhere else, along with his mind.

"Do you want to just lay down together? We don't have to do anything else. I would love to just lay in your arms again like old times."

Jarrett sighed and said that he couldn't wait to have me in his arms later, but he was interested in something else right now. I didn't know what he was talking about, until I did, and I was trembling with need. He picked me up and set me on the edge of the table we'd just had dinner on. My body was shaking, and my skin was full of goosebumps. His fingers ran down the sides of me, then up my skirt, and pulled down my panties in one clean motion. "I love that you're still wearing skirts."

I didn't mention that I'd put it on because he was around. I still wore them around the house for comfort, but this particular one was in hopes that he would do what he was doing now, lifting it up and touching what was underneath. I loved the sound of his intake of breath when he felt how wet and needy I was. "You are ready for more it seems."

I agreed, not saying anything, except to whisper his name when he opened my legs and moved in between them. I asked him again what he was doing, and he just shrugged, telling me that he was having some fun. "I need a taste."

My eyes closed and I knew then that I was in for some pleasure. Jarrett's mouth was intense, and he was far better at it than he had a right to be. I could already feel my body tensing up in anticipation. I couldn't even feel his breath on me yet, but I knew it was coming and the anticipation of it was almost as good as real life.

Jarrett went to his knees, pushing mine open further. He didn't need me this wide, but he liked to tease with air and cool breath. I was squirming after only a few moments and Jarrett asked me if I was ready. I wasn't, but damned if I was going to admit to that.

His mouth came down on me, heat swamping my senses and I tried to jerk away. It was my first reaction, and it was a strong one. My body convulsed away from him, and he merely brought me back to the edge of the table. There was nowhere that I could go, and he stood up after a moment. He bent over me and seemed to have better control over me. I was shaking when he was only a few licks in. My legs tried to close multiple times, but Jarrett wasn't going to have any of it. He pushed them wide and sucked on the sensitive parts of me that begged for him.

Since I couldn't keep my mouth shut, Jarrett's hand went there and shut me up. I was still whining deep in my throat, trying to get away from his lashing tongue, but to no avail. Jarrett had me right where he wanted me and there was nothing I could do about it, nothing I wanted to do about it.

When it all became too much and I'd came multiple times, I begged for the rest of him. As much as I loved the feel of his hungry mouth on me, other parts of him were just as ready for me. I grabbed a handful and pulled him close. Jarrett knew my buttons, but I knew his as well.

Harboring Doubts

Jarrett

I woke up with a start from the loud noise coming from the other room. It took me a minute to orient myself and to remember where I was. I got a smile on my face when I saw Antoinette next to me, and then it clicked that the loud noise was a kid crying. I can't say that I'd woken up to that sound before. It was quite something. I started to wake Antoinette up, but she was so peaceful. I figured I would let her sleep. It couldn't be that hard to get him back to sleep. Atticus was easy going.

When I got in the room, I approached the crib with unsure steps. I had no experience with kids whatsoever and they were a bit intimidating to me. Antoinette was so easy with him, and I could tell she was a good mom by the way they interacted. I tried to focus on what she had said and done before to soothe him. It couldn't be time for him to be up, it was still the middle of the night, so I hoped he would go back to asleep easily. He'd only been asleep a little while.

I held the boy when he reached for me, and I swore it hit me in the chest when I pulled him up close. He had the biggest eyes that were the same color as mine, His expression was open and when he smiled, like his mother, the whole room lit up. "Wow, you look a lot like your mom."

Atticus made some sounds, nothing concrete and I sighed. "Who else do you look like?" I whispered the words softly, more to myself. I saw a few pictures floating around of her ex-husband. I remembered him and he looked nothing like the kid. I would hate the guy, want to kill him for touching her, but he was dead, so I didn't even get that satisfaction.

The boy was sleepy-eyed, so I put him down back in his bed. I was feeling some kind of way about it all. My hands were shaking a bit when I backed out of the room. I stood outside the door in the hallway for several minutes, not sure what to do next.

I was torn in a few different directions. I wanted Antoinette badly. The time that we spent together was always amazing and that feeling that I'd held onto for so long, was back in full force. I didn't think that I could feel this way about Antoinette again, not after everything that had gone on between us, but the truth of the matter was that I wouldn't be able to stop, even if I wanted to.

I couldn't stop the intrusive thoughts either. When I looked at her son, I didn't know who I was looking at. He was the product of a relationship that I didn't want to admit happened. I didn't know how I was supposed to pretend like nothing happened right after I left. The math was clear, he was born way too close to when I left. She must have started dating another guy while we were together or a few days after. I'd run the numbers many times since I'd found out about Atticus, and it made me come to the same conclusion. Antoinette hadn't waited even a few seconds for me to leave before she was on to the next.

It made sense. Antoinette was so sexual. She was just as needy as I was, every time. It was one of the many things that I loved about her, but I could see how that could become problematic. It still hurt though, even if I did understand it. It tore me up inside when I thought about it. Seeing Atticus made all those feelings come to the forefront of my mind and I truly wasn't sure what to do with it. I would have done anything to stop the racing thoughts that came.

I stood outside the child's door for quite a while. I thought through my options, knowing that if I stayed there, getting back into bed next to Antoinette like nothing had happened, wasn't really something that I saw as feasible to do. It made no sense to me, none of it did and I had to process that. I needed time to get myself together. My emotion regulation always seemed to be a little off kilter when it came to Antoinette.

I decided that I had to get out of there for a while. I'd come here for her, had her and now I had to go. I know that it wasn't going to be the best reaction when Antoinette woke up and I was gone, but that was better than the subsequent conversation that was going to happen if not. She had gotten defensive before and though I got it, I still wasn't going to be very happy about it. We needed some space, or I was going to say something that I regretted.

Some of my things were back in the bedroom, so I went to go get them. It wasn't like I was going to be able to go anywhere without my boots. It was a mistake to go in there though. As soon as I stepped in the darkened room, I saw Antoinette lying in the bed, part of her luscious body was bare for me to see. I wanted to go to her, lay down next to her and pull her in close. I knew that it wouldn't take long at all to get Antoinette in the mood, even from complete sleep. How many times had I pulled her in against me when I was hard, only to have her wake herself up and rub herself up against me in a way that I wasn't able to stop? It was madness and I wanted more. My whole body was shaking with need. It had been so long; I'd just gotten her back. Why did I have to go anywhere? Why couldn't I stay and curl up against her like I wanted to?

The desire was there, but I remembered Atticus in the other room and all the questions that he raised. I wasn't ready for that conversation, and I didn't know how to do one without the other. I cared too much about Antoinette to only use her body for my needs. I wanted so much more from her, and I knew that anything short of everything, wouldn't do.

So, I left. It hit me a little harder than it should have to leave the two of them behind. I knew that it was the two of them that I walked away from. It wasn't just Antoinette anymore. I had to think of her and Atticus as a pair. That was hard to do, but I knew that it was that way or nothing. Was that why I was leaving, because I didn't know if I was willing to accept both?

**

I got a call from Nathan when I was getting into my vehicle. It was perfect timing because if he had called me sooner, it would have woken up Antoinette and I would have faced questions of why I was leaving in the middle of the night like I was. I don't know what sort of answer I would have given, but I can guarantee that it wouldn't be a well-received one.

"What's up?" It was late and I could tell that Nathan had something on his mind.

"How are you doing? I've been trying to get ahold of you."

I wasn't paying attention to the calls that I'd gotten earlier. I'd heard the phone buzzing on Antoinette's nightstand, but I had no desire to stop what I was doing at the time. When I really listened to how Nathan was talking, I realized that he thought I was in trouble or something. I told him that I was fine. I wasn't sure why he thought otherwise.

"Well, when you didn't answer, I just started to think the worst, you know? You have been through a lot. I saw you when you came out of that mountain tunnel. I know what they did to you. I know that you have every right to be tired of dealing with it."

I stopped him and told him that he didn't know what he was talking about. "I am fine, Nathan, really. I am just leaving Antoinette's place and honestly, I don't think you had anything to say to me that I was interested in at the time."

Nathan made a sound of surprise. "You are with Antoinette?"

I sighed, "Well, I was. I am still trying to get used to the fact that she is a widow with a kid now. A lot has changed, and I am still getting my head around it."

"It's been hours. I figured that you'd have your head around it by now."

I paused and then laughed, "That part always came easy to us. It's the other part that is complicated."

Since Nathan was up and I wanted someone to shoot the shit with, we decided to meet up. I wasn't ready for what came next with Antoinette and maybe bouncing my thoughts off someone else would help. It couldn't hurt. Alone, I was already wearing my head out with it all. I needed a break.

***

"So, tell me what is going on with you?" We were at Nathan's place and even though it was three in the morning, he had a beer waiting for me when I got there.

"Not much. I am trying to get my life back, but it's taking longer than I'd hoped."

"You just left Antoinette's place. That sounds like you are moving right on along. I am glad to hear it."

I was glad that I had gone, but there was another part of me that wanted more. It wasn't enough that I had her in my arms, I wanted more for us. "I don't know what is going to happen with Antoinette, but she is what has kept me going all this time. I put her up on a pedestal. I know that she isn't perfect, not one is, but it is taking more than I thought to wrap my head around what happened when I left. How can I trust her now?"

That was the real gist of it. I wanted to trust her, so that we could have a real life together, but how could I if she would be so disloyal days or weeks after I left? She never waited for me, even before she knew that I was missing. Antoinette was sorry for what happened to me, so was that all last night was, a pity fuck? I liked the idea of that even less and I had to get out of my head. Nothing good was going on in there.

"Most guys in the military say that you really can't. We're gone so long, and it's hard for women to wait. I don't think that is the case. You weren't married or anything. It was a fling from what you told me."

It was a fling. We got together one night and just didn't separate until we had to. We talked, laughed, make love all the ways we could. It was intense, it was enough to keep me going for over a year when I was taken. All of it pointed to more than just a fling, but it was on a superficial level. It was our souls connecting in a way that I never had before. I couldn't just put it in such a flippant category.

"It was more than that."

"For you. You don't know what it was for her."

He was right, I had made some assumptions. I wanted to believe that she felt the same, but did she? Antoinette felt good back in my arms. Why couldn't that be enough? It certainly was enough last night.

Ominous Foreboding

Antoinette

Jarrett was touching my body ever so softly and I backed up against him. I could feel how hard he was, how much he needed me and there was nothing I could do to stop the yearning that took over. I rubbed back against him repeatedly, trying to get that sexy sound that he made one more time. I could hear it in my ear and my body vibrated.

"What do you want Antoinette, tell me?"

I wanted him and I told Jarrett that he was all I needed. "I've waited so long for you. I love you, Jarrett. We made a baby together and I want you to fill me with another."

Jarrett growled into my ear, telling me that he was going to do that very thing. "I'm going to keep you full of babies, so that you can never leave me."

I told him that I wasn't going anywhere. I could feel his hand reach around and rub the very spot that was trying so hard to get attention. It wasn't exactly the sort of feeling that I wanted at the moment, but it was good enough for me.

My moan made him growl a little lower in his throat and that sound was going to be the end of me. It wasn't long at all before I was begging Jarrett to get me out of my misery. I was red hot, and I knew that only his touch, his kiss, his hard need was going to satisfy the craving that I had for him. It was hard for me to focus on much of anything lately, because I couldn't stand how badly I needed him. I begged Jarrett again to take me and make me his.

"I can't."

I turned to Jarrett and asked him why that was. I was saddened by his answer.

"Because I'm not real."

I frowned and then touched his face gently. "You seem real enough to me."

He chuckled. "That is because you're dreaming of me, Antoinette. Wake up."

I sighed and said that if this was a dream, I didn't want to wake up. My face was curled up into a smile and when I opened my eyes, I was still just inches from getting everything that I wanted. Reality wasn't as kind to me.

I woke up with Atticus fussing that he was done laying down for the night. I probably could have slept a little longer, but that was simply because I had stayed up too late with Jarrett. I looked over to the spot where Jarrett was supposed to be. He was not there. I was a little stricken with that information because I wanted to see him badly, but I didn't jump to any conclusions. He was likely somewhere close by, and I would see him later. This is what I told myself anyways.

I thought of Jarrett in my dream and how he was seconds from pressing in and making me moan in pleasure. That was what I remembered most from my dream world, and it was the one part that I clung to. I wanted to go back to that. I needed to feel Jarrett's hands on me again.

This wasn't to be. I had to get up. Atticus wasn't bawling like he was hurt or hungry, but he was certainly annoyed at me for taking so long. I called to him from the other room as I got dressed, telling him that would be there in just a moment. That seemed to slow down the grumbling, but it certainly didn't take it away.

I went into the next room to Atticus and asked him how his night was in a sing-song voice. He was always such a happy child. I almost asked him out loud if he knew where Jarrett was. Worse than that, I almost called him his dad. I definitely couldn't let that slip out. I almost had. It was never my intention to keep it away from him at all. I never thought I would see him again and now I didn't know how to say it. It was a lot to deal with. I don't know why I was so afraid, just that I was, and the words kept getting stuck in my throat. Not today though. I would tell Jarrett everything today.

After a quick check through the rest of the house, it was unfortunately clear that I was here by myself. Right or wrong, I would have expected more out of Jarrett. I can't believe that he just left in the middle of the night, especially after everything that had gone on between us. How could he act like nothing happened? He didn't even leave a letter, nothing. I looked. I was annoyed by the whole thing. I just wanted to see him.

Part of me was glad that I hadn't told him about Atticus. If he was taking off in the middle of the night, it was probably best to keep my hopes down. It seemed quite obvious to me that whatever I thought was going on between me and Jarrett, wasn't. I thought there was something more, or maybe that there could be more. He had gone through so much and he talked about how he thought of me the whole time. So why after all that, why would he be so quick to leave? I thought we had a really good time together. Was I wrong? Jarrett had me reconsidering everything. I didn't like feeling this way, not one bit. Usually, I knew where I stood, but this time around, I honestly had no idea.

Atticus started fussing, feeding off of my own feelings. After the night we had together, I was devastated that I woke up alone. I shouldn't be, Jarrett made no promises, but it still hurt. He made me feel like something was happening again between us. Maybe he was just really good at what he did.

Instead of waiting around and dealing with my own feelings, I decided to go see Ashley. She would be able to help me make sense of it all. This was all just more complicated than I would have hoped. Nothing at the moment made any sense at all. Why did Jarrett leave and why was I so devastated by it?

I got Atticus ready to leave and tried not to see the resemblance to his father. Usually, those eyes made me feel better, like Jarrett was still with me in a small way, but now I knew that he was back and just didn't want to have anything to do with me. I wanted him to do as he had before, stay and crave me like I was a bad habit. What happened? Why did he leave?

The questions swirled in my head as I finished getting everything together to go. I couldn't just walk out the door anymore. I had all kinds of things with me for Atticus and beyond that, I was frazzled from lack of sleep and why I hadn't gone to bed early like I usually did. Jarrett really did a number on me, and I wonder if he would ever know how much he decided my mood and outcome for the day. He had such a hold over me and I swear it was like he didn't even know it.

Atticus was in an especially good mood, nothing but smiles and he pulled me from all of my fretting. Jarrett was gone, but he would be back. If I had learned nothing else, it was that Jarrett had a way of coming back to me. I just had to be patient, long after I'd lost hope. This time it wouldn't be so long at least. If it was, I don't know if I would be able to handle it again.

I packed Atticus into the car and got in. Something felt off, so I made sure that I had everything with me that I needed. I couldn't figure out what I'd left and then I went through the house to make sure that there wasn't anything that I'd left on. I don't know what gave me this strange feeling inside of me, but I had to push it down. Whatever was the cause, I had things to do today, and I couldn't let my unsettled feelings get ahold of me.

Giving Ashley a call before I took off, I told her that I would be there in a few minutes and that I was on my way. I had to stop and grab Atticus a snack because there wasn't much for him at home, but that was it. I would be at her place in ten minutes tops. We had plans to go through some new pictures that just came in and I was excited to see what was captured on a trip we'd went on not long ago. I was excited to see her and to get her opinion on what was going on. Ashley always knew what to say and I needed that now.

***

The ill feeling I had compounded as I took off out of the driveway. Everything was more intense, sounds, smells and even the colors my eyes could see. Time slowed down and I was freaking out. I almost pulled over and I was only a block from my house. Something inside of me kept telling me that I needed to turn around and go back. I don't know what it was, but I didn't listen to it. People usually describe me as someone that felt too much. I tried to be analytical, but I couldn't help it.

The feelings I had usually made the decision for me, but today was different. Today I was pushing it all aside and blaming it all on Jarrett. Him leaving left me off.

I should have known better. There had been several times in my life where I listened to my gut, and it had saved me from a lot of grief. This was one of those times where I should have listened. A couple of minutes after I left, the rain started to come down and it was way more than seemed possible. It hadn't been sunshine when we left, but there certainly wasn't storm clouds in the sky. I slowed down and made sure that I was paying attention to the road more closely. Atticus must have felt my negative energy, because he started to cry.

I shushed him, trying to calm him down, so I didn't worry too much about how slow I was going. I was around a four-way, when I heard screeching tires and then the sound of crunching metal. My head went sideways, hitting the top of the door and it took me a minute to realize that we were upside down. I could hear Atticus crying and upset. I wanted to turn my head to see if he was okay, but I couldn't move. It hurt to move and black tinged the edges of my view.

Before I could figure out if Atticus was okay or not, I started to black out. I knew it was happening and I prayed with my last moments thought to make sure that he would be alright. He needed an angel while I went to sleep for a while. I was so tired all of a sudden.

There was a sound in the distance, someone trying to help, asking If we were okay. I tried to answer, but nothing came out. At least now I knew that my son was going to be alright. That was really all that mattered, so I could rest more easily with the news. I wanted to stay present for my son, but at least others were there and would help him. The sounds, the rain and the pain, all fell into the background.

Bonds Unexpectedly Formed

Jarrett

It was the second time the phone rang, and the number was one that I didn't recognize. Antoinette had called me earlier, likely when she first got up and I hadn't answered. Now, someone kept calling from a different number and when it stopped ringing, I looked the number up and it said that it was the hospital. I had no idea why they would be calling me, but my attention was on it now. Who could it be?

When the number called again, I did answer, and I was stopped in my tracks with what I heard. "Do you know a woman named Antoinette?"

It took me a minute to put it altogether. "Yeah, I know Antoinette. What's up?"

"You're the last number in her phone. She was in a car accident, and she has a young child that was with her at the time of the crash."

My radar went on high alert. "Atticus, is he okay?"

"Yes, he is, but she is not. She is in a coma, and we were hoping that you would come take her son. He needs to be fed and it would be easier if someone that the baby knows picks him up. Or if you could steer in me in the direction of someone who would."

It took only a minute to realize what needed to be done. I needed to go there and pick him up. I didn't know what to think of what I'd heard, Antoinette being in the hospital, but I knew I had to help. There were a lot of conversations that we hadn't had, and I didn't know who to call her family or friends. I knew her husband was dead, so that left one less person to contact. "Okay, sure. I will be down there in a few minutes. Is Antoinette going to be, okay?" I couldn't help the tinge of panic in my voice.

The nurse on the line paused, "She is in the best hands and seems to be a fighter."

I agreed that she was and told her that I would be down there in a few minutes. I was breathing heavily when I put down the phone. I felt grief and regret. I couldn't help but wonder, what would have happened if I had stayed, instead of getting lost in my own emotions? I'd gotten out of there quickly because I was overwhelmed with everything, but now I had to know that all of this could have been avoided, if only I hadn't left like I did. If I had woken her up, made love to her again, maybe she wouldn't be in a coma now. I blamed myself and the self-loathing was intense as I drove over to the hospital.

The nurse from the telephone call recognized my voice and took me to Atticus. He was upset, but for some reason, as soon as I picked him up, he started to calm down. It was like he knew that I was here to make everything better and he accepted it. I wasn't too enthused with the job, but he seemed to know exactly what was going on. I was calmed by his presence, instead of the other way around.

The nurse asked me if I knew anything about babies and I admitted that I didn't know much.

"Well, I am shocked he isn't yours. You know that he looks just like you."

I was stunned by her words, and I waved them off. She must have been seeing something that wasn't there, because she expected it to be there. That had to be what it was. I think. I don't really know what was going on, but there was something to it because when I looked at Atticus, I swear I could see my own eyes looking back at me. He really did look like me, if that was what I was looking for. Now, after hearing her words, he had an uncanny similarity.

We stared at each other for a while, before I took him for a walk down to the guest shop. I needed supplies, like some kind of stroller. I knew that I was going to have to go to Antoinette's place eventually. I had her keys with me, as well as some of her other belongings, but a part of me wanted to wait until she was conscious. I wanted to be at the hospital when she woke up, but after a few hours, it was clear that Atticus needed his bed and his own things. He was grumpy and I told the on-call nurse that I was taking him back home. I left my number so that they could call me if anything else happened. I grabbed a few things from the hotel and went to stay at Antoinette's. It was strange to be there without her, especially when everything that ran through my head was what we had done together the last time that we were here together.

It was different to be a child's caregiver. I didn't know what to do at first, but with some internet searches and pure guessing, I was able to figure it out pretty quickly. It wasn't all that hard to focus when there was nothing to do but spend time with a baby. I wasn't sure how I would feel about it all, but before the night was out, I was absolutely enamored with the little one. I know that he was the root of my angst coming back, but Atticus was such a delight, it was hard to be upset about any of it.

The next day I called up the hospital and Antoinette was still out of it. She had come-to for a few minutes, but they'd immediately sedated her because she was so upset and incoherent. They hoped that the next time she woke up, she would be easier to manage. I didn't think Antoinette would ever fall into that category.

**

Nathan called the third day that I was watching Atticus and while I tried to blow him off and tell him that I wasn't interested in a visit, I finally had to invite him over to Antoinette's place. He didn't know about the wreck, so I had to relive it by telling him.

"Man, you two seem to have the worst luck."

I always felt that about myself. Obviously, I had been taken in by rebel forces and tortured, but I had never considered it with Antoinette. She had a heck of a time with her luck as well. She got with me, I took off for over a year, got married to another, he died. She might have the same level of bad luck that I had.

"It would seem so."

Nathan made a similar comment about Atticus that the nurse had made. "You know, he really does look like you. He could easily be passed off as your son."

I thought that he was off, but then he said something about how it would be easier if I wanted to get with her and have Atticus as a stepson.

"Woah, you are moving too fast for me, Nathan."

Nathan waved me off. "You love her, and she is going to come out of this looking at you a little differently. You should take the chance and stop pretending like you don't want her as your wife."

He was right, but I wasn't ready to hear it. I wasn't ready to think about marriage, family, though what was I waiting for? I was out of the military, something that was good for having a family. Is that what I wanted? A few days ago, I was running away from the very idea of it. Having Atticus around changed my thinking. Almost losing Antoinette pushed my thoughts in another direction as well.

"I don't know what I am going to do when she gets back, but I know that I am going to miss this little guy." I wasn't being dramatic either. I really was going to miss the little boy. He was sweet and he had me wondering what could be different. I worried about how I was going to feel when he was back with his mom. I didn't want to go ahead and pretend like he meant nothing to me. I couldn't have that. He and his mother meant more and more to me every day. I don't know how I was going to work with all of that, but I was going to have to do my best to figure it out.

"I mean it, Jarrett. He looks a lot like you. Are you sure he isn't yours?"

I waved him off and told him that he shouldn't say things like that. I wanted the boy to be mine, but he wasn't. It was just wishful thinking. I wanted to think it was a possibility, but she'd gotten married. "No, Antoinette would have said something if he was. I think he just looks like me because I want him to."

"No, the kid really looks like you."

I ignored his words and tried not to see the resemblance more than I already did. It wasn't something that could be fixed easily, so it was better to pretend like I didn't see what I wanted to.

Nathan stayed for a while, but eventually I got a call from the hospital and Antoinette was awake. I was ecstatic to hear that she was doing better, and I got her son and his things together to go up there and see her. Antoinette was likely going to be missing her son desperately, so I wanted Atticus there to cheer her up.

As I got him ready and then myself, I worried about what Nathan had said. I worried that I would lose them both and now I had a stake in keeping both of them in my life. Atticus was so cute it was hard not to love him, and Antoinette well, I'd loved her since I heard her playing in that cafe. She was every bit of perfection that I had come to love about her and there was no going back. I couldn't stop myself from loving Antoinette now.

I was full of all kinds of emotions as we made our way to the hospital. I tried my best to think positively. Atticus really could pick up on the emotions of the people around him and I didn't want him to pick up on anything bad. He was about to see his mom, so that was really all that mattered. He still asked for her quite a bit and I felt bad every time I had to tell him that she wasn't there. I knew that she wanted to be, and I was so glad that I would be able to reunite the two.

We took the elevator to the second floor where the ICU was and it was a big relief to be there, knowing that she was getting better. I held Atticus a little tighter to me and I liked the feeling of him against me. I had really grown in the role of his caregiver, and it was going to be lonely without him around. I don't know what I was thinking, but I knew that I was ready to see Antoinette again. I missed her and she really was a sight for sore eyes.

Antoinette smiled big when I saw her. I don't know if she was looking at me or Atticus like we were the greatest thing she'd ever seen, but it didn't matter. I couldn't get over the smile that fell across her face. It was contagious and I had to remind myself that we weren't sure what was going on with us just yet. I had already projected my life with her and Atticus in it. It was going to take a long time to make it so, though I knew now that was the direction that I wanted to go in.

Antoinette's face fell after a moment, and I couldn't for the life of me understand why she looked so stricken. I asked her if she was okay, and she shook her head.

On the Cusp of Life-Changing News

Antoinette

For the longest time, I felt like I was in one big, long dream. I went from one dream to the next, as they got crazier and crazier. Usually when I dreamed, I didn't remember, but this time I remembered all of it. I also remembered that I wasn't alone in the room, people would come and talk to me, though I can't remember what they said. There was this strange feeling of being in my body, but not being able to control it. It was a weird feeling, and also a scary one. At some point, I realized that something was wrong with me, but I didn't know what and I didn't know how to fix it.

The worst bit of my dream state was I kept dreaming about a car crash. I dreamt about it repeatedly, so much so that it was easy to figure out that the wreck was likely real. It felt too real to be a dream. That realization made me fight the dream state, while before I just wanted to stay in it. It was nice there, not a lot of worries, but that got me thinking that I needed to wake up. Life was never meant to be peaceful.

I did finally wake up, but I was still very confused. I woke up in a low bed, with bright lights above me. It didn't take long at all to realize that I was in the hospital, which made sense because I did get in a wreck. My head was covered in bandages when I moved to touch the tender spot. It freaked me out to feel the woven material. I didn't know how bad it was, but I wanted to focus. I needed to remember what happened to me.

About the time I was trying to replay the last moments that I couldn't remember, a nurse came in to check on me, and she looked surprised to see me, but her face recovered quickly, and she asked me how I was feeling.

I wasn't feeling very good, everything was stiff and hurt more than anyone should. I relayed those feelings to the nurse, and she smiled empathetically. "It's because you were in a car wreck, and you were knocked around pretty bad. I'm glad to see you awake. They were starting to worry about you."

I was worried about myself as well, so it's not like that was hard to understand. As bad as I felt, it didn't seem possible that I could stay upright, but my bed was sat up and she asked me if I could. I tried, but it was harder than it looked.

"That's good for now, you're sitting up. Don't try to walk anywhere yet. You had a heck of a blow to the head, so your equilibrium is probably going to be off. It's been over a week since you've been here, so your body is going to need to be reminded how to move. The fact that you're talking well is a good sign. I'm going to go get the doctor, so he can check you over."

I told the nurse I was grateful, and I would wait for the doctor to tell me what all was going on. I was sitting back, trying to calm myself like Nurse Betty suggested, but another thought occurred to me that had me sitting up straighter in the hospital bed.

I called out to the nurse as she was leaving, "Wait, what about my son? He was in the car with me. Is he okay?" I held my breath waiting for an answer.

As I asked the question, my voice broke, and the nurse at once came back to me to soothe me and told me that everything was fine. "I recalled the last person on your phone, and he came and picked up your son. He's also came up here a couple of times to see you and had the baby with him. He does very well for a new father. They look just alike."

It was alarming to hear someone say what was the truth. I knew that he was the father and that they looked exactly alike, but Jarrett didn't know that yet. Was he starting to wander and guess? It wasn't that hard to imagine. Atticus really did look like his dad.

"He doesn't know he's the father. I haven't been able to tell him yet. He just got back from the military not too long ago."

I tried to explain the situation, but without context it was almost impossible. The nurse assured me that everything was going to be fine and that she would give him a call as soon as she was done talking to the doctor. "He will bring your son up here and then everything will work out. I have faith that this is all going to work out for you. The hard part was waking up and here you are."

I waited in the bed for someone to come back and see me. The doctor was an elderly man about sixty or even older and he had a very nice smile on his face. He was the sort of doctor that made me feel better as he came into the room, because I knew then that I was in good hands. The doctor took a look at my head and my eyes, and he told me that everything was looking good. I'll be the first to admit that I questioned the validity of his assessment. I felt utterly horrible, but apparently it was going to be that way for a little while. He expected me to make a full recovery and I liked to think that he was right.

"Did the nurse go ahead and call my friend to get my baby?"

"I was told that the call had been made and he said he would be down here soon."

Of course, the first thing it made me think was I was going to see my son. The second thought was I was going to see Jarrett and I don't know if I was ready for that yet. We hadn't left on the best terms and the reason why I had run off was starting to come back to me full force. Jarrett left and I had a hard time dealing with it.

He had been taking care of my son and I didn't know what was going to happen when he came. I was more nervous than anything else. Had he figured anything out? There's only so many times that he could look at our son and not see it. It seemed to be clear to everyone else when they saw the two of them together. Maybe he couldn't see it, but that could only be for so long. Soon enough, he was going to realize that it was like looking in a mirror.

Then, what was he going to think? I should have told him when he came over, but everything happened so fast. I didn't regret what happened between us; I couldn't, but there was a lot left unsaid. I think the timing of telling him was going to come up.

The nurse came in to ask me what was going on. "What do you mean?"

"Your heart is going crazy, and the doctor thought you were in here exercising or something. Are you okay?"

I looked at the monitor. The numbers didn't really mean anything to me. It was making a sound, flashing, but I didn't feel it any sort of way. "I am nervous, that's all."

"We can tell anyone that is here to visit that you don't want to see them. Maybe it wouldn't be for the best in your condition. You just woke up and I don't want you upset."

I sighed, "The guy that has my son is what has me nervous."

She looked shocked, but when I told her a tiny sliver of our story, she was just as nervous as I was. "And he really doesn't know?"

I shrugged, still not believing that I'd told Nurse Betty the truth, before I had the courage to tell Jarrett. I think I wanted to get a reaction from someone that didn't matter as much.

"If he doesn't know, he should by now. He has had him for a week, and they look just alike. I assumed he was the father."

We didn't get to say much more to each other, because the man in question was finally here. I heard Atticus a moment before they came through the door, and they were surely both a sight for sore eyes. I was still getting used to seeing Jarrett again. He was like seeing a ghost and I don't know when that feeling of relief when I saw him was going to go away. I'd thought for a very long time that I was never going to see him again. Now, he was right here in front of me.

Atticus made his desires known and that was to come over to me. He climbed up onto the bed with my help and I hugged him to me. "I've missed you."

His smile was sweet, and I broke down in tears. It wasn't because of how badly I missed him, because I did miss him. It was because I could immediately see what the nurse and everyone else saw. The two were just alike and Atticus looked like his dad. It was even more evident when the two of them were right next to each other.

Jarrett appeared to be full of nerves. He wanted to know how I was feeling, and I could barely meet his gaze. The last time we'd spoke, we were making love, then he was gone. That sinking feeling was back, but this time it was for another reason altogether. I had to tell him, finally. It had to come out and though I wasn't sure how he was going to take it, I had to get it out.

Nurse Betty said something about how she had some rounds to do and though I knew she did have work; Betty didn't want to leave. She knew that there was drama about to happen here. Since I'd already been told by the doctor that I was going to have to be here for a while, I knew that I would be around to tell her what was going on. I wanted to mention that but couldn't. She was just going to have to wait to hear how it all went down. I wasn't even sure just yet how it was going to finish.

After the nurse was gone, there was a silence between Jarrett and me. I think that neither one of us was too sure what to say. I knew that I was at a loss for words and the hush stretched on around us.

"I am sorry I left." Jarrett said it quickly and it took me a minute to play it back, to understand what he was talking about.

"I am sure you had something important to do." I was holding Atticus, making faces and trying hard not to smother him in hugs that I wanted to rain down on him. I missed him so much. Even in a coma, I had felt the loss of him.

"I freaked out and ran off."

"Oh," the words came out with more emotion than I wanted. "I see." I didn't see. What was he freaked out about?

Our son? His son. I had to tell him. He was going to be so mad. He still didn't know.

"I really am sorry. It makes me think that if I would have stayed..."

I waved him off and told him that he shouldn't think like that. "I don't blame you, so you shouldn't either. I was just going to a friend's house. Yes, I was going to gossip about you, and you being gone, but the accident was just supposed to happen."

He looked at me strangely. "Supposed to happen? How do you figure that?"

"Well Jarrett, there is something that I have to tell you. I should have told you before, but now is better than any other time. I just have to say it." I hesitated. Could I really get the words out? They felt stuck in my throat, but I had to tell him. It was time.

Bonding Over Truths

Jarrett

I watched Antoinette struggle with her secret and at some point, I almost told her that it didn't matter, just because it was so hard to watch her struggle in the way that she was. Whatever it was she had to tell me, couldn't be that dramatic, but then again, maybe it could be. She was holding Atticus, and it was weird not to have him after watching him for days. I could feel the loss already.

"What did you want to tell me? If it isn't that important, we can wait."

She said that it was important and before I could get more information, I tried to see what it was that was going on. She wasn't saying anything that made sense. I could hear Antoinette giving herself a pep talk, but nothing came out.

"It can't be that serious."

Antoinette smiled slightly, "I wish it wasn't. I'm sorry, I'm really not trying to drag this out." She took a deep breath and then said something that was going to literally change my life forever. Here I was saying that it couldn't be that dramatic. I was eating my words now.

"Atticus is yours."

"What?" I thought I'd heard her wrong because my mind was breaking down trying to wrap around what she'd just said. There was no way that what she said was true, right? It made no sense. The math hadn't made sense before, but now I knew that it did. I looked at the boy that I'd taken care of for days and I saw it. I think I saw it a while ago, but I didn't want to hope. It was hard enough to think of her having a kid with someone else. Now that she said he was mine, I didn't know how to respond. I was happy in one instance, but not in the other.

"Atticus is your son."

"Why didn't you tell me before?"

I didn't like that she hadn't told me, though I could see from her expression that the tone I used could have been better. She snapped her head around to look at me. She wasn't pleased with me at all. I could see that although I wanted her to understand what was going on between us. I don't know if she actually did or not. "You have been gone a while. I just found out that you were still alive."

She was right, but I could have known this before now. I have been taking care of Atticus for days and I didn't know he was my son. I wouldn't have left. I should be happy about this, so why wasn't I? Why was I mad?

"I don't know what is going on here, but you could have told me before now."

Antoinette agreed, "But there was a lot going on and I didn't know how to tell you."

She was imploring me with her eyes, but I ignored it. My emotions were up and down and since the nurse had to come in because her blood pressure was too high, I decided that it was best for me to leave the situation. I didn't know what to say to her. I was upset and she was as well. I needed a few minutes to breathe.

Since I was questioning everything, I went to the one place I'd avoided but knew that I had to go. I was going to go back home. My mother was still around, we talked on the phone every week, but it was time for me to go see her. I went to see her after my long absence, but also because I had to know if what Antoinette said was true. Was Atticus mine? Did he look like me when I was younger? I wanted to show mom the pictures I'd taken of him. I wanted to know if it was possible. I felt like it was in my heart, but I needed someone else to agree. I needed to know for certain that what Antoinette said was real, even though I knew it was.

When I got to my parents' house, my father was away, which was just as well for me. We didn't get along and since I'd gotten hurt, just as he feared when I enlisted, I was happy to see my mom only. She always had a smile for me and since I hadn't been home in a long time, I got an extra-large smile that always made me feel welcome.

After the initial shock of seeing me, mom wanted to know what had been going on and she was one of the only civilians that I told the truth to. I couldn't lie to her if I wanted, plus, I didn't want to. I trusted my mom to tell me what was really on her mind. I tried my best to focus on what she said, even though my mind wasn't on what it should be. She wanted to talk of the torture and the time away, I wanted to talk about what I looked like as a kid.

Finally, I was able to cut into the conversation that I wanted to see pictures of myself when I was a baby. Even though I tried to make it seem like it was just a natural part of the conversation, I could see that wasn't to be.

"Why do you want to see your baby pictures? You got some girl saying that she has had your baby while you were away?"

She said it with a smile on her face, but she quickly stopped that smile altogether. "Are you serious? I was just joking."

I nodded my head, "Whether you are joking or not doesn't matter. That is exactly what is going on and just you saying that is kind of freaking me out."

"Well, do you think it's yours? I mean, is the timing right?"

My mom was always the one that thought of everything with a clear mind. Here I was freaking out inside, which made thinking straight a thing for another day. I didn't want to go there with her, but I needed her clear mind. She was already getting into the back of the closet where her pictures were located.

"Yeah, it is. I think. We met a few weeks before I shipped out and it is a real possibility."

Mom stopped; her lips trembled a bit. I know that she always wanted a grandchild, and I had on many occasions told her that it wasn't likely going to happen. I think she was getting her hopes up. Those same dark eyes that I saw in the mirror and when I looked at Atticus, looked back at me through mom. "Do you think it's yours?"

I was going to put her out of her misery, when she showed me a picture of myself about a year old. It was about the same age as Atticus, give or take a few months, and I was the spitting image of Antoinette's son. I knew already that he was mine, but I guess I wanted to see it one more time to make sure that I was right.

When I took the phone out of my pocket and showed her the pictures that I took of Atticus, she started to get teary-eyed, and I knew that he was mine. My mom had already claimed him and wanted to know when I was going to bring him over.

"Well, I don't know, because we just got into it."

"Didn't you just say that she was in a coma?" Mom asked me, confused. I could see how she would think that, but she wasn't there, she didn't hear how it all went down. I was told offhandedly that Atticus was mine and I hadn't taken it well. I expected her to come out with it, no matter how awkward it was going to be.

"Yeah, but I got upset that she didn't tell me right away. I stormed off, basically."

I couldn't look at my mom because I knew what her cool brown eyes were going to show me. They were going to make it clear that she thought I was an idiot, but I already knew as much. I wasn't but a few feet into the hallway before I realized that I wanted to turn around and go back to Antoinette. Pride is what kept me going and then I came up with coming to see my baby pictures, though I already knew.

"I thought I raised you better than that, son."

I was a disappointment to her and that cut me like a knife. "You did, I just wasn't ready for it."

She sighed, "Well you only get one time to react, and she is always going to remember that. You need to go back up there and make it right. I want to see my grandbaby and I won't be able to if you mess things up."

I could tell where her worries lay, but I was worried about something else altogether. I wasn't worried about if I could see Atticus, Antoinette would never keep me from him. It wasn't in her. I wanted the two of us to be together. That meant that I was going to have to really make it up to her and I had handled it badly. Mom had a right to be mad at me.

I was just about to tell her that I was going to fix it, when the phone rang, and it was the hospital. At first, I thought it was going to be something wrong with Antoinette, so I answered nervously, but it was Antoinette herself. She didn't say much, but the few words she said were enough to throw me off even more than before. This was real.

"What did she say?" Mom wanted to know when I got off the phone.

"She wants me to come get Atticus. She has some physical therapy to do and thinks that it would be good for me to get to know him."

Mom smiled and said that I should come there after I picked him up. "Where am I going to stay?"

"There is your old room," She suggested with hope.

I waved it off. "I will find somewhere to rent. It sounds like I am going to be around for a while."

Mom was happy and I was too, though I wasn't going to show it. I still had many questions, but now I was going to get to know my son, as Antoinette put it. She didn't mention how I'd acted, but I could tell that she wasn't impressed. I didn't blame her either. I could have managed it a lot better than I had. I would do better next time.

When I got to the hospital, Antoinette looked tired, and Atticus was happy to see me. There was something in the way that he reached for me that made me think it was all going to be okay. I didn't want to think about the alternative, and everything really was going the right way. She accepted my apology and even gave me a smile when I told her that I would come see her every day until she was out of there. "Our son missed his momma last time. I want to make sure that he doesn't miss you this time."

"Our son. I like hearing you say it."

I nodded my head in agreement. I really liked saying it, it turns out.

On the Verge

Antoinette

I'd been in the hospital for over two weeks now and I was ready to get out of here and go home. Jarrett brought Atticus to see me every day, but it wasn't enough. I missed him and it wasn't right to be apart this long. I was healing, the physical therapy was helping in all areas, but it wasn't happening fast enough. When I was finally released, I was more than ready to go.

Jarrett came by at eight in the morning like he promised, and he, at once, let Atticus down to come to me. He started walking more, and now I watched him with awe. In only a couple of weeks, he'd changed and grown so much. Was that what having his dad around was like? Did it benefit him that much?

"Are you ready to go?" Jarrett asked me, taking the bags out of my hands. I had several therapy instruments to help me along and he had his hands full.

"Yeah, I can take some of that."

"No, I got this. Atticus will hold your hand."

I wanted to pick him up because that was what I was used to and when he took my hand and started to follow Jarrett, a tear came to my eye. Why did I feel like he had grown up so much and I'd missed it all? It wasn't a good feeling. I was beside myself with emotions. Jarrett's hand went to the back of my arm, comforting me without saying a word.

When we turned away from the drive to my place, I asked Jarrett what he was doing.

"We're going to our place."

He didn't say his place, he said ours. "What?"

He sighed, "You didn't think that I was going to let you go back to that apartment, did you? It isn't nearly big enough for the two of you, let alone the three of us. This place is more suitable for a family."

I don't know when we decided to be a family, but I didn't mention the discrepancy. I did have to say something though. Jarrett was making a lot of assumptions. I always said that I wouldn't want a man that told me what to do. It honestly wasn't so bad. I liked where he was going with this, but I didn't want to make my own assumptions. This could all just be to help me out. Jarrett was spot on with character.

"A family?"

"Yeah, me, you and Atticus. I am back home, and I am not going to let you all be away from me. I have to be here to protect you."

I really liked the sound of that, but I was trying not to fall into his arms. We had a lot between us to work out. It wouldn't be that easy.

"I don't know if we need a protector, but Atticus sure does need a father. I would have told you sooner."

"You did tell me pretty quickly. I could have handled it better."

If that was his apology, it was about as shoddy as mine, which seemed to be right on par. "Can we just pretend like none of the last year and a half happened? I am just back from the mission, and I've missed you."

I saw the desire in his eyes, and I reminded him that we had things to do. "Maybe we can have that reunification later."

His dark eyes held mine. "Promise?"

I paled with his sudden attention and wasn't sure how to feel about it. Jarrett was messing with me, and I don't know if he was aware of it or not. When we got inside the new rental that Jarrett had obtained, I looked around. Atticus was ready to get down and when he did, he shot off towards his room. He motioned me to follow, and I was amazed at how cozy it looked even though they'd only been there a week or so. How did he get it all done in that little bit of time? He must have been working hard on it. It was sweet and everything that Jarrett did was a way of welcoming me.

"Where should I put my things?"

Jarrett motioned to the bedroom, and it was clearly the one that he was staying in. His coat was laid off across the bed.

"In there?"

He chuckled, "It's not going to bite you. Yes, in there."

I must have had one hell of a look on my face, because Jarrett knew exactly what I was thinking. He was taking this all so well, like we were overnight this perfect little family. I was going to take more convincing to believe it. I wanted to fall into Jarrett's arms, but we had a lot between us. "Do you think that's a good idea?"

He scoffed, "I would never do anything you didn't want to do. I know you need to heal, and we need to get to know each other again. We have time now."

Time sounded very nice. The hospital had a way of making a person question if they had time left or not. I certainly needed more of it. I didn't think I would have more time with Jarrett and now we had all this time on our hands.

"You aren't going to get mad if I'm not in your arms and underneath you tonight?" I asked the question quietly, so that only he could hear me. His eyes widened and he pressed his lips together.

"Why did you have to say it like that? Of course, I am not going to be mad Antoinette, but I am definitely going to think about it for a while though. You didn't have to..." His voice trailed off and I think I'd broken his brain. He looked like he was never going to be the same again. Why did I like the way he acted so much? I liked knowing that he wanted me that badly. It did something for my ego and also brought a lightness between the two of us that we really needed. Everything was always so dramatic, but now there could be something else.

***

Getting back on my feet took more out of me than I thought it would. I still had to go to physical therapy a few hours a week, but most of it had to be done at home. Jarrett would assist me with certain stretches that were supposed to help, but all it did was awaken parts of me that called to him. It wasn't long at all, before I was purposely asking Jarrett for help, even if I didn't need it, just so I could get his hands on me.

Atticus was down for a nap, so I had no shame in rubbing myself back against Jarrett as he helped me. I heard his sharp intake of breath and knew that he was feeling the desire just like I was. We were both very suggestive when it came to the other, so I knew that I didn't have to say much of anything, my body was doing all the talking that was needed.

"Are you messing with me?"

His body was molded to mine and I was now leaning forward, his hard knot pressing against the back of me. I knew when I felt it what it was and how much I wanted to feel him inside of me. It was killing me, especially because I'd experienced how good it felt before. The two of us together really were perfect.

"What are you talking about?"

I stood up and broke the contact. His eyes were a bit glassy when I looked back his way. I asked him if he was okay, but I knew what was going on. He was hard, it had been weeks since we'd been together and even though he was a man of patience, it had to be gnawing at him. It was starting to wear on me, but I still didn't know if I was ready yet or not.

"Do you want me to find someone else to help me with stretches? I am sure I can find someone..."

He quickly told me that wouldn't be necessary, and he had a dirty look on his face with just the suggestion. "You will not ask anyone else for help. I am here."

Jarrett's eyes met mine and held them in his grip. His tanned face was chiseled with good looks and his generous mouth reminded me of all the great things he could do with it. I wanted to feel him against my flesh again. I was tempted just as we stood there, but it wasn't the time. I wasn't ready, was I?

My breath came out faster as he leaned in for a kiss. Right before our lips touched, he promised that it would be just a moment and it was, but those few seconds set my whole body aflame with desire. Jarrett kissed me like his life and mine depended on it. He grabbed the side of my face and pulled it in, pressing his hard body against mine. Every inch of me was molded against the available inches of Jarrett's body. I was shaking when he pulled away, his tongue retreating. I was left standing there, chest heaving and my whole body atingle.

"Now, back to the stretching."

I sighed, wondering when exactly the tables had turned but knowing that they had. I didn't want to be the one that was helpless against my need, but I was getting there quickly. Living with Jarrett gave us way too many opportunities for things to move beyond the point of no return. There were too many times in the day when he was so close that I could imagine him touching me and where that touch could lead. I was obsessed with how badly I needed to know the extent of his desire for me. I couldn't stand the idea that it wasn't as high as mine.

So, I messed with him and then he would do the same to me. This back-and-forth flirting was coming to a head. That kiss in my opinion, brought us right over the edge.

Jarrett helped pull my arms back and it was done by him being behind me, pressing up against me in the most erotic way possible. I was standing there focused on the stretch itself, but I should have known that I wasn't getting away unscathed. The kiss had damaged my focus, while his hard body now pressed against me was there to take down the last of my barriers. If I agreed to it, Jarrett would be down in seconds to give me what I needed. It was I that kept putting it off. He was simply making it harder and harder to do so. That was his intent from what I could see, and he was doing a good job of making it impossible for me.

When Jarrett bent us both down, we were in a position that I liked very much with my clothes off. I bumped my ass back against him and he growled, "Who is messing with who now?"

I acted innocent, before I rubbed against him for several moments, making us both sweat. When I moved away and looked behind me, Jarrett's face was slack with lust and his eyes were all black, no pupils in sight. I think maybe I'd gone too far, and I wiggled free from his grasp before he changed the trajectory of the day.

"Get back over here."

I giggled and told him that I thought exercise was over for the day. It certainly hadn't gone the way I wanted it to, but it was good enough for me. Jarrett was now on the same level that I was, though looking at him watching me didn't settle well with me. Jarrett reminded me of a caged animal, dying to get out and get his way. I was what he wanted, and it felt like he was willing to do anything to make it happen.

"You can flirt around here messing with my head all you want Antoinette, but you have to come to bed sometime."

The reminder of where I slept was nothing new, but it felt like it had almost a threat attached to it. Why did I want it to be a promise?

Giving in to Temptation

Antoinette

Maybe it was because of what Jarrett said earlier in the day, but I dragged my feet all night. We'd done exercises around six and there was several hours left until bedtime. They usually were filled with activities that just made the time fly and it was bedtime before I knew it. Tonight, I made sure that I took my sweet time, and I prolonged it as much as I could. Atticus went to bed an hour later than normal, more likely because I was too nervous to be alone with Jarrett. He'd made his intentions for the evening clear, and I wasn't ready for it. Well, I was, but I was also overwhelmed and nervous as hell, so postponing his attention sounded better than anything else.

Now, the time had arrived for the two of us to lay down and I was shaking inside. Right before I went into the bedroom that Jarrett was already in, I decided to beeline it to the bathroom. I could take a shower and get myself together.

I had my clothes off and was stepping into the hot stream of water, when I heard the door open behind me and I knew who it was. Jarrett was here and he wasn't going to let me run away, not without a chase.

"What are you doing? You already took one this morning."

I scoffed that he knew that and called me out on it. "I felt a little sweaty."

Jarrett's form was moving but the curtain didn't show me what he was doing. I was too nervous to move the curtain back and see for myself. I always got this way when I was around

Jarrett. He had this draw over me that I couldn't control much at all.

"What are you doing?" I could no longer see him and then when I did, I took a step back and gasped.

"There you are. I get a feeling that you were trying to run from me, and we can't have that."

He was stepping into the shower, making me move back from his strong body. The scars on his chest were new and I still hated to see them. I put my hand to them, but Jarrett wasn't here for anything sweet and cozy. He, at once, had my hands entwined in his and then behind me on each side. It was clear when he pressed me against the wall, pressing me between him and the shower tile, I knew he was telling me without words that I wasn't going anywhere. I wouldn't have moved an inch if I could have.

Jarrett's body may be scarred up a little from his time in captivity, but it was still as strong, muscular and sexy as it had always been. "I am not going anywhere."

His hands were on either side of me and our kiss deepened. Every second that his lips were on mine, I felt closer to him. I was already so close to melting into his arms. I never wanted the moment to end. I wanted more, but the sensation was hard to pull away from.

He was the one that stepped back and made me look at him. I wanted to know why he was stopping, even if I didn't quite have the words for it. They were stuck in my throat, and I was sure that nothing was ever going to be the same again.

My hands encircled his neck as he lifted me up and pressed me against the tile. I was pushed up against the hard part of him and it would have taken nothing for him to slip inside. It was tempting to lift back and slide him in. I knew that I could, it wouldn't be difficult at all, but I wanted another kiss.

Jarrett's lips were almost as enticing as his hard need, though likely I was trying to prolong the anticipation just a little while longer. I was on the cusp of something great and all I needed was a little more time. I rubbed myself against him, listening to my own sounds of pleasure that couldn't be stopped.

"Are you ready for me?"

I agreed that I was, not really thinking it through. I knew what was going to happen next, but I wasn't prepared mentally for it and called out loudly. Jarrett's name was like a curse on my lips, and I couldn't stop the moans that came when he pressed hard and fast inside. He was deep in seconds, my body stretching to accommodate his size and my eyes were closed, focused on the most intense pressure I could imagine. It was all more than I could take, and I clung to Jarrett as he throbbed inside of me.

Our lips met repeatedly, and I whimpered when he finally started to move. I swear he had grown, but I never got to get a word out before his strokes were faster and even more devastating than before. All I could do was hold on tight as wave after wave of pleasure rolled through me. I'd never felt so sensitive before, and I swear every thrust in was like the first. My inner sheath clung to him, just as my arms and legs did the same.

At some point I let go and slid down the wall partially. I wasn't able to keep up, so he turned me around and pulled my ass out enough to slip back in without much complaint. Now I didn't have to hold onto anything. Jarrett kept us both upright with his long length pushing in and out of me. All I had to do was feel, which was great because it was all a bit overwhelming. I tried my best to focus on my own pleasure, but it intensified and burned me up. I called out his name several times, every wave bringing more and more pleasure.

"I thought of doing this every single night when I was gone Antoinette."

I pushed back from the tile, and it made his thrust go deeper. I couldn't help the shaking that my body started to do. Jarrett had no idea what he did to me. He wreaked havoc with my systems, and I never wanted him to stop. I curled one arm around his neck, and we kissed before I was moved back down to take him his way. Jarrett quickly reminded me that he was in charge.

"Where are you going?" His words were raspy in my ear, and I admitted seconds later that I wasn't going anywhere. His hand snaked around to my center and played there as I tried to wiggle out of his grip. There was something so perfect about the way he held me and maneuvered my body. I couldn't help how completely I gave myself to him.

"I am not going anywhere Jarrett. I'm yours."

He must have really liked the sound of that, because he pushed deeper and finally filled me with his hot seed. I felt it slide out of me and down my leg, before I lost myself completely. He prolonged my orgasm, rubbing hard and making me beg for mercy. I think that was what he wanted, chuckling in my ear and making me shiver even more. "It's even better than I remember."

I didn't have an answer. I didn't have anything to say, and I was likely not going to be able to walk out of there on my own.

I'd run away from Jarrett into the shower and now he was here with me and there was nowhere I could go. I was stuck here with him and when he started to kiss me, making it clear he wanted more, I suggested that we go lay down.

He laughed, "Are you sure you don't want to hide from me anymore?"

I sighed and pushed him on his chest. Obviously hiding from him wasn't going to do me any good. Jarrett made the point that there was no running from him. "Would you let me if I wanted to?"

He picked me up and slid in with one fell swoop. I called out in pleasure and clung to his neck when the let go of my waist. I gripped him tighter and it gave Jarrett the free hands to do as he pleased with me. I thought that he was taking me to bed, but he drilled me against the tile until the water ran cold and my arms were shaking with the effort to hold on.

When he finally settled me down on the bed, I was too comfortable for much else than sleep. My body stretched like a cat and if you listened hard, I bet you could hear me purring. Jarrett tried to get my attention, pulling me in against his bare chest and rubbing my skin with his gentle hands. I felt languid next to him, but I was done, and he must have realized it, because he let me drift off to sleep moments later.

***

When I woke up, it was light outside, and I thought that I was on my own. I didn't know how I'd made it through last night. Jarrett had a desire that was so much more than my own and it was overwhelming sometimes. It felt like he had so much sexual energy within him, that it drowned me every time.

I looked over and saw that Jarrett was watching me. My cheeks at once got red. "I didn't know you were awake too."

"I haven't slept yet. I've been waiting for you."

It didn't take much of a guess for me to figure out what he was waiting for. His dark eyes were hungry and followed me when I moved. Had he not had enough? I shivered again with his attention. "What were you waiting for?"

He hauled me up to him, my legs straddling his waist in no time at all. It was as if they knew exactly where to go, one on one side, and then the other on the other. Jarrett wasn't wearing anything and since he was rock hard, standing up proud and full, there was no denying what he waited for. I was sore and tired but found myself pressing down to get his reaction when I did.

I wanted him to moan, and he did. His eyes got big, crushing fingers dug into my skin at my hips and he buried himself inside of me. Neither one of us could do much more than close our eyes and feel the connection. He was huge and throbbed deep inside of me. Even though I was on top, there was no way that I had any control. Jarrett moved me with his hands on my waist, as well as thrusting from underneath. Every flick of his hips moved me and I fell quickly into the pattern of before.

Jarrett played me like a fiddle, and it was hard to have no say over my own body. He could make me feel like I was on top of the world, or down in the dumps. Every time he moved inside of me, my emotions soared with the pleasure I got from him. I'd never felt so connected to another person in my whole life. It was impossible for us before, but now, I can feel how this could work. I had faith in Jarrett and me. With Atticus, we could be a real family.

Blissful Announcements

Jarrett

"Do you know what today is?" I asked Antoinette as she rode me slowly. It was pretty routine for our mornings together, but this day I was being ignored.

I moved my thick need deeper inside of her, holding down her hips so she couldn't run off like she wanted to. When I moved inside of her and made her whimper, I knew she was close. Antoinette was always thirty seconds from a proper orgasm. I was a little jealous that she could derive so much from only a few strokes, yet my ego was made large by that ability often. I could never go back to the old way of doing things, being with any other woman wouldn't do. Antoinette spoiled me in all ways and riding me every morning was one of those ways. I had made some decisions for today and I wanted to show her the next change we needed to go through.

"Seriously, what's today?"

Antoinette whimpered. She was held down, I was throbbing inside of her, but it wasn't enough to take the edge off. Antoinette made it clear that she wasn't happy with how things were going and wanted all of me. She rocked and clenched me, which made me thrust up once. I gasped, she whined and clenched me again. Antoinette wasn't happy about me holding her back, and she made sure that we both paid for it. Her vice-like grip only made me lose my control just a little bit more.

"Do you really not know?" I prompted Antoinette once again.

Antoinette sighed, and then shifted her hips. Why wasn't I ready for that? I almost popped out of her, and I once again had to settle in deep to keep her in place. She called out, pushed her eyes closed and shimmied on top of me. Antoinette came hard, shaking on top of me and there was nothing I could do to stop it. All I had to do was pull free, but that was literally impossible. How could I do such a thing when her lovely folds held me so lovingly?

I slammed upwards until we both called out in bliss. I knew that I was going to lose myself, but she was going to come with me as well, so it was all worth it. Antoinette collapsed on top of my body, and I took advantage of that, holding her down while I frenzy-fucked her until submission. She wanted to be the one that held on, instead I was the one that ruled her in the end. It was only a small win, but enough that I felt satisfied when I pulled free of her hot core. Antoinette moaned with loss, and I was immediately prepared to go right back where I started. I would have, if her hand on my chest didn't stop me.

"What are you going on about?"

Rubbing up against her from beneath, I told her that today was special, and I wanted her to know it.

"What is so special about today?"

"Two years have gone by since we've met."

Antoinette asked me if that was true. I agreed that it was, and she said that it felt like a lot longer had gone by. I tended to agree with her. I'd lived a whole lifetime in those two years, went from wanting to die, to dying to live. It was amazing what could happen in such a short span of time. I would never imagine the time to be insignificant again. Antoinette would always remind me that everything could change in a couple of years.

"That is a long time."

"It is."

"Well do you want to celebrate?" Antoinette was still on top of me, and I was growing inside of her again. She whimpered when I started to move, telling me that wasn't what she was talking about.

"I can't think of a better way. Can you?"

Antoinette's eyes were already closed as I moved in and out of her quickly. She just braced herself and let me do all the work. This was not going at all how I thought it was going to go. I thought that I was going to turn to her and pop the question. Antoinette would be surprised and then we would make love. I didn't realize that stopping would be the problem. I just felt so good inside of her that I never wanted it to end. I was never going to get the question out, if I couldn't stop pushing deep.

She rode me when I tried to stop and took us both to the edge of reason once more. I told her that I loved her and since I'd said it before, Antoinette ignored the implications of my words. She had her hands on my chest, eyes closed, doing her best to get off one more time.

"I love you Antoinette," I told her again.

She didn't say thank you, but she didn't say she loved me either. Antoinette was focused on catching her breath. "I mean it, Antoinette; I love you so damn much. I don't know what I would have done without you."

Antoinette scoffed, "You would have found love with someone else."

I stopped her and made her look at me, "Do you really believe that?"

The smile on her lips died. I was getting too worked up, I knew it, but there was nothing that I could do about it. This was the moment when I was going to ask her to marry me. I swear I would command it if I thought it would work.

"I don't know. You know how I feel about fate. It sounds good, but I don't know if I believe it or not."

I scoffed and held her hips down, driving up. "I could never find this with anyone else. It's not like I haven't been with my fair share of women before."

Antoinette called out and pushed up against my chest. "What are you saying?"

"I want to marry you Antoinette, that's what I'm saying!"

Antoinette pressed back, but my lower half was steadily driving into her repeatedly, doing my best to get the feeling that I was looking for. She called out my name and I didn't stop, waiting only until it was a mantra on her lips. Then and only then was I able to focus on anything else. When she was exploding above me, then I asked her again. This time, I made sure that there was no doubt about what I asked.

She didn't answer me for some time, and it was only when I stopped completely that Antoinette finally listened to what I had to say. There was something in the way she looked at me that stunned me to silence. "Do you really need an answer?"

It was a strange time to be asking such a thing, but it wasn't my intention. I thought that we would have this sweet moment, but everything went to the next level when

Antoinette slipped me in. I couldn't focus on anything else when I was inside of her and I'm pretty sure that was the point. I tried to push her away, but I couldn't. "Yeah, I want an answer."

She clenched me and made me call out. She was so tight, suffocating my length with her desires. "There is your answer."

Before I could get to the bottom of her answer, Antoinette popped off of me and left me all messed up. I had already come once, though I could admittedly go again if given a chance. With Antoinette, I was never too far away from getting everything that I needed from her touch. When I reached for her, Antoinette giggled and moved her body out of my reach.

"Before I give you an answer to your question, I have something I have to tell you. I was going to tell you soon, but it hadn't come up yet. Now is a good time."

She had me worried when she said that she wanted to tell me something first. Did that mean something bad? Was there something she'd done that I wasn't going to be able to accept and she wanted to get it out before the marriage?

"What is it?"

Antoinette pressed her lips together and while it was a serious moment and she was obviously bothered by whatever was on her mind, all I could see was the long lines in front of me that called me. I swallowed hard and even though she'd already drained me dry, I was dying for it. What more could I ask for? "I'm pregnant."

I thought for a moment that I hadn't heard her right. There was a lot of noise going on in my mind, but after I heard her words, everything got quiet. "Wait, what? Are you serious? Atticus is going to have a little brother or sister?"

Antoinette nodded with a smile and my eyes took another look at the body I stared at for hours on end. I should have seen the changes sooner, but I wasn't looking for them. Maybe she was getting a bit thicker in the middle, her breasts were a bit larger. When I touched them and sucked on her nipples earlier, Antoinette had practically jumped out of her skin. At the time I figured that she was just primed up and ready to go, but maybe it was more than that. Maybe it was something else.

"Well?" Antoinette's voice told me that she wasn't too happy with me for something, though I really didn't have any idea what she was talking about.

"Well, what?"

"What do you think of me being pregnant?"

It never occurred to me that she would be worried that I wouldn't be thrilled. I moved to pull her back into my arms and though she started to straddle me, I stopped her. "I love that you're pregnant and we're growing our family. I thought you would know that. You've made my life what it is and before you, I didn't care about anything. Now, I have Atticus and you. Adding more love to our lives can only be a good thing, right?

Antoinette nodded with a tear in her eye. "I was really nervous that you might not want another child."

I waved her off, "Not hardly. I can't wait. I missed a lot with Atticus, but now I won't miss a thing. I couldn't ask for anything better. I have you, him and more to look forward to. How could it get any better than that?"

Antoinette sighed and we kissed. One minute I was thinking about how great it was going to be to grow our family and the next minute, I wanted to practice making more. I was never going to get enough of her pristine body on mine. Before too long, Antoinette was positioning herself where I needed her to be and then everything went downhill from there. No more talking, no more listening, just movement, grunting and orgasms.

Later when neither one of us had any more energy to continue, Antoinette finally gave me the answer that I was looking for. I should have known that she was going to say yes. I guess I did in a way but hearing her say it was a different feeling altogether. We held each other for the longest time and Antoinette fell asleep in my arms. It was the greatest feeling ever. I couldn't get over how badly I wanted her next to me for the rest of my life. Now, there was even more to celebrate. I pulled her in tighter when I thought of the fact that she was carrying another one of my children. I couldn't wait to see her all big and pregnant. I knew that it was going to be a sight and I couldn't wait. The anticipation was high as I held her in my arms. This was the first night of the rest of our lives and I was ready to begin.

I kissed the top of her head and tried to slow down my racing thoughts. With Antoinette by my side, the world was ours.

A Storybook Wedding

Antoinette

There was a buzz in the air, and I couldn't help the smile that filled my face. It was hard for me to focus on anything, especially because today was the day. I was finally going to marry the man of my dreams, and the father to my soon to be two children.

Atticus was dressed up proper in a baby blue suit and I couldn't stand how cute he was. He'd just left out of here with Jarrett's mom and he was too cute for words. I wanted him to stay, but I did have to get ready. Today was the day I'd thought about for years. I never guessed that I would marry a man I'd met at a bar or one that I wouldn't see again for so long. I also didn't think that I would get married again, but this was right. This was what was supposed to happen all along.

I heard a knock on the door of the room I was using to get ready. Ashley came in and she had a big smile on her face. "I can't believe how beautiful you look."

I thanked her and turned so that she could zip me up. I was determined not to lose my cool. It was easy to do. I wanted to cry, and I don't know if I was going to be able to make it down the aisle in one piece. I am pretty sure I was going to lose myself before I even got there. Everything inside of me was sure that I was never going to be the same again.

"You look scared."

I waved her off, "I'm not afraid of Jarrett or the wedding. I don't know what it is. I guess I am afraid of things going right. I won't know what to do with myself."

That got a chuckle out of Ashley. "It's going to be okay. You two are meant to be together. Everyone around you two can see it. I've been talking to some of his friends, and they are all surprised that he is getting married. They didn't see it happening before, but now he is in bliss, and I think they are all jealous. I know that when I see him looking at you, I'm a little jealous myself."

I waved her off, but I knew what she meant. Jarrett looks at me as if I may very well be the last woman on earth. I catch him staring at me sometimes and I am overwhelmed by the intensity that he shows. It fills me with desire and need, but also a feeling like I will be unconditionally loved forever. Nothing really tops that feeling in my opinion.

Ashley helped me push a few strands of hair out of my eyes while we talked, and she slicked it back. I already had my hair done and I was glad for the help. I don't know how the lady got my hair to sweep up as high as she did. It was nice to have the pampering. Jarrett treated me extra special as of late and I really enjoyed it. Once I told him that I was pregnant again, he's been a dream. It made me realize how different this pregnancy was going to be. Jarrett was by my side and that was all I needed. He was amazing and showed me what I was missing.

The wedding was rushed to accommodate being done before I was waddling down the aisle. Before I could really focus on anything else but the dress and cake, Jarrett had a wedding put together. Usually, it was the bride that did all of the work, but not this time. Jarrett wanted a say and he wanted to take the stress off of me. When I suggested that we get married later after our daughter's birth, Jarrett didn't want to hear it. He was much more convinced that it had to be done right away. It was sweet and he really did do most of the work, so here we were. I was showing, but not as much as I'd worried. I didn't want it to be so obvious that I was pregnant. In the end it didn't matter, and the day wasn't going to be any worse because I was pregnant. It was a celebration of more love and a growing family.

Ashley walked me out since we were close, and my own family wasn't around because of the short notice. Since we'd been friends for so long, it almost felt right. I tried not to think about what others thought. It was my day, not theirs. I saw Jarrett at the end of the line, and he had nothing but love in his eyes. Atticus was up there with him and now they were like the spitting image of each other. They were wearing the same color tuxedo to accentuate their dark skin and eyes.

My smile grew as Atticus ran to me. He wanted me to hold him and of course I had to. It was a very important moment and I wanted him there with me. I walked up to Jarrett, and he grinned. Other men might be annoyed, but not Jarrett. He nodded like it was the right thing to do and helped me with Atticus when he started to get a little wiggly. We were married and sealed with a kiss in front of everyone. Our family felt complete now more than ever.

***

The ceremony was over, and the reception started with Atticus being laid down for a nap. He'd been so overstimulated with everything going on and being in the middle of it, that it was good to let him rest. I lost Jarrett for a while, though I quickly found him over by some of his old unit.

When I walked up, everyone congratulated the two of us and I was touched by how many of them came to support Jarrett. There hadn't been a lot of time and notice given, but his whole unit came anyway. I'd enjoyed hearing about Jarrett and how he had been before we met. He apparently was a reluctant womanizer before I showed up on the scene. I couldn't envision that, simply because he'd always been mine since we met. When he was gone I'd missed him, but when he was with me, he gave himself so fully that I couldn't help how complete he made me feel.

"I am just glad you guys could make it with such short notice," I found myself saying to Nathan. He was staying locally, and I felt like he had something to do with everyone showing up.

"We wouldn't have missed this for anything. Many of us wanted to meet the woman that kept him going. We all talk about how we need an Antoinette in our life. Your inspiration is well known."

I waved Nathan off. He made me blush, but it was in a way that I couldn't quite put my finger on. All of the men in his unit were great specimens. They were all well trained, well groomed and physically dominating. It was hard not to feel some kind of way in their presence.

"I know it means a lot to Jarrett that you're all here."

Nathan told me that they were all alive because of him, so it made sense that they owed him a visit.

"How is that?" I had heard many stories about Jarrett's time as a Green Beret, though none of them ended with him saving the whole unit. I wanted to hear it, just so I could know Jarrett a little bit better. I wanted to know everything there was to know about him.

I looked around for Jarrett, he'd walked off to get more drinks. Nathan was smiling at me when my attention was back on him. "He held out for weeks. Jarrett didn't know that we were stuck where he got taken. It was almost two weeks until we were able to get out of there and they never came for us. I don't know how he did it, but he held out through something so horrible, so that we could get out of there in one piece. Everyone here owes their life to your husband. Being here really is the least we can do."

There was a wave of pride that filled me. Jarrett was my husband and from everything I'd heard about him, he was a man that I should feel proud to be with. He was already such a great dad to our son, and I know he was going to be amazing to our daughter. We'd only been married for a few hours, but we'd lived together for a while, and I knew what sort of bliss I had ahead of me. It was hard to regret anything.

"Wow, he never told me any of that. Does he know?" I felt like if he knew something like that, he would have shared it with me. I don't know if that was true or not, but I would have loved to have told him so that he could feel the same pride that I did for him.

"Of course he knows. We told him when we all came to visit him in the hospital. He was jacked up pretty bad and none of us thought he was alive. Jarrett has been surprising us ever since and when we heard that you two were getting married, there was no way that I would miss this for the world."

I hugged Nathan and thanked him for telling me more about my husband. "You have a good one," he told me. I agreed, I knew that Jarrett was the best. There were some instances where we didn't understand each other and they were hard to get through, but at the same time, I was learning so much. I was so happy that all of his friends were here. I got to hear and see another side of Jarrett.

When he came back over, everyone broke up and he asked me if I wanted to dance. Since it was our wedding reception, I took him up on it and let him glide me around the floor for a while. He was just as light on his feet as I thought he would be. Jarrett must have done something, because the next song on was ours. I smiled at the sound of it.

"This is the first time that we've danced together and it's our song," I said out loud.

"Yeah, what do you think of it?"

I told him that it felt perfect, and I meant it. Everything about this day was surreal and when I was in his arms, I couldn't feel any other way. I felt like I was home. That's what Jarrett was to me.

I settled my head against his chest as we danced to a slower song. He held me ever so softly in his arms and before I could focus on anything else, I knew exactly what was going to happen next. "Do you want to get out of here?"

Jarrett's voice deepened and I could tell by the timber of it that he wanted to get nice and close together. It wasn't hard to see. His eyes were dilated, and his need was never too far from his face.

"There are a bunch of people here, Jarrett." I tried to remind him that we'd invited them all and we couldn't take off.

"Just for a little while. I must have you now, Antoinette. Don't make me wait."

His eyes drew me in and before I knew what I was doing, I was following him to a nook or cranny that we could find to be alone. I giggled like I was a teenager. Jarrett made me feel like anything was possible with him and he filled me with such excitement. I was never going to get enough of it.

Choosing What Truly Matters

Jarrett

Epilogue

One Year Later

The picture in front of me was perfect. Antoinette was nursing Brianna and Atticus was eating his breakfast, while he practiced repeating words of things he saw. It was a game that he played with Antoinette, and I was still surprised when he learned new words almost every day. Antoinette was a great teacher and mother. She was really hitting her stride with the two of them and I'd never seen her look more serene. A part of me wanted to watch her all day, even though I had a meeting I had to get to in a while.

"What are you looking at?" Antoinette asked me. I was staring and my attention had been pulled away.

"My beautiful wife."

I must have had a twinkle in my eyes, because Antoinette shook her head and told me that there was not time for that this morning. "You have to go meet with Nathan, remember?"

I agreed, but then I reminded her that I could always be a little late. I am a civilian now. I could be late and there would really be no repercussions. I was still getting used to civilian life, but the freedom was amazing and still hard to adapt to.

"Jarrett, I mean it. You are not showing up there late and all disheveled. We did that at our wedding reception. You're not going to do it again. What would people think?"

I leaned over and kissed her. "That you're amazing."

She scoffed, "They already know."

"When are you going to be back? Truth be told, I already miss you."

"It won't be too long. I don't know what Nathan is coming by for. Maybe he just wants to catch up. I haven't really talked to him all that much. I don't know what they are up to lately."

"You're nervous?"

I shrugged, Antoinette could already read right through me.

"No, I just don't know what he called me out of the blue for. Don't you wonder?"

Antoinette shrugged, "It will be good for you to see an old friend. Why worry about anything past that?"

I sighed and said that she was right. How did Antoinette always seem to get to the heart of the problem so quickly?

"It will be good to see him. It's been a while."

She gave me a kiss and told me that it was going to be fine. "We will be here waiting for you when you come back," Antoinette promised me before giving me another smooch.

"How are you going to be waiting?"

Antoinette took a step back and looked at me with mischief. "Well, time it right and it could end well for you."

"I am going to set my watch for nap time."

Antoinette giggled and agreed that it was a good idea. She always gave me great incentive to get back to her. Was that her plan all along? If so, it was going well.

***

Nathan wanted to meet at a bar a few cities over. I wasn't familiar with it, but it wasn't hard to find with directions on my phone. As much as I tried to focus on what he was talking about, my mind kept drifting to Antoinette back home.

"Are you even listening?"

Nathan's face wasn't angry, but he was frustrated. "Sorry, my mind is on something else."

"What?"

I told him that he didn't want to know, but that wasn't the answer that he was looking for.

"Why not?" Nathan snapped back.

"Because you just divorced your wife and don't want to hear about my perfect marriage."

Nathan made a face and agreed that he didn't want to hear about that. I knew that he was looking at me as if we were the same, but I could tell that Nathan wasn't doing so well. What was he here for? Was he just trying to get some time talking? I wasn't sure what was going on, but I told him I was listening, and I apologized for losing focus before.

"Are you two happy?" Nathan wanted to know. It had been a year and I think I was happier now than I'd ever been before. Antoinette was a dream and I held onto my time with her tightly. I knew intimately that I could lose it all if I wasn't careful.

"Yeah, we're happy. You will find someone else Nathan."

He waved me off, "You know that is likely not going to happen. If I stay with the military, it will always end the same way."

I agreed. Military life wasn't made for families and relationships. The problem was that we got used to the adrenaline rush of battle. It was hard to walk away from that. If I didn't have my family here, Antoinette to hold me down, I don't know if I would have been able to give it up. I said as much to Nathan, and he brightened up.

"That's why I am here."

I was confused about what he was talking about, and I asked him to clarify.

"I'm here to see if you were ready to come back. The unit misses you and we could use you back."

I thought he was joking. I laughed a little, but it was when I realized that he wasn't joking that I started to sober up. "Sorry Nathan, but there is no way."

He wanted to know why. "Don't you want to save people?"

I agreed that I did, but now I worried about people a lot closer to me. "They are who I protect now. I don't want to lose them, chasing that next high. I miss that feeling, really, I do, but I'd miss Antoinette more. I can't leave her again. I won't."

Nathan didn't look so upset. He took a swig of his beer and mumbled something about how he didn't blame me. I could tell his own marriage dissolving wasn't helping. I asked him if he was okay, and he gave me an earful. As I was listening to it, I only grew more thankful for Antoinette. Without her, I don't know what I would do. I never wanted to go back to my life before her.

We talked for a while longer and when I finally left for the night, I was ready to get home and get Antoinette back in my arms. Being around Nathan, seeing how sad he was and how much he missed his wife, I held her a little tighter when I got home.

She took the extra love without a second guess. "You okay?"

I said that I was, and Antoinette pulled me in for a kiss, telling me that she'd missed me. "I figured that he was going to try and talk you into coming back to the unit with him."

Pulling back, I asked her how she knew that.

"You are amazing. Of course they want you back. They thought that it was going to take longer for you to get better and now that you have, they want to use you again."

I was always surprised that Antoinette seemed to understand situations much better than she should have. I agreed that it was what Nathan wanted. When she didn't ask me what I had told him as an answer, I was curious why that was. "Don't you want to know what happened? You didn't even ask me what I told him."

Antoinette shrugged, "I figured that you told him you have a family now and civilian life suits you."

It did and that was basically what I had said. I never knew how Antoinette knew me so well, but I nodded. "Something like that."

Antoinette grinned. "I know that you weren't leaving us."

I looked at the clock on the end table and Antoinette agreed that I had came at the right time. "Your timing is impeccable soldier."

A shiver ran through me as I watched her take to the bed in front of me. She didn't have much on, like she was waiting for me and by the time she got to the top of the bed, she had nothing on at all. My body started to hum in response and Antoinette giggled when I looked at her a certain way. I was there, longing for her and when she crooked her finger at me, I moved forward without a word.

She stopped me at the edge of the bed. "Too many clothes."

I growled at her, not ready to bare myself to her. I wanted to get my hands on her bare flesh, not worry about my own. If Antoinette got her way and was able to touch and tease me like she wanted, I would never be able to hold it together as long as I wanted to.

She knew that too. Her eyes held mine and I shivered. I knew exactly what she wanted to do to me and when she clicked her tongue, the clothes came off. Many people would think that I was the one in charge in our marriage. I liked to believe I was, but I knew better deep down. Antoinette ran my emotions, and she usually knew exactly how to get her way.

Antoinette was on the top of the bed, looking up at me, beckoning me forward in a way that I couldn't refuse. I shook as I made my way over her body. I stopped when our lips were close, and her body lifted up to meet mine. I sighed as I kissed her, knowing it wouldn't be long at all before I was buried deep inside of her.

Our lips and tongue entwined, as our bodies did the same thing. Antoinette didn't waste time with anything else. She opened her legs to me and immediately made sure I was able to slide my way in. I called out loudly as I moved inside of her, choking on her desires. Antoinette had this hold on me and from the start, I was never able to turn away.

I held her gaze as I filled her up, until her eyes closed in pleasure. I was never going to get sick of the look on Antoinette's face when she hit her limit. Her body shook and before too long, there was a big part of me that was finding it hard to hold back. Antoinette's nails dug into my skin. I swear she was trying to drag me back down with her. I tried to fight it, but it did me no good.

Filling her, I kissed Antoinette and stopped the whimpers that escaped her lips. It was a sound I was never going to tire of. There was no way I could leave her again. When I thought of the unit, I missed them, the camaraderie and the opportunity to save people, but what I had with Antoinette was something even more important. This is where I was supposed to be.

A while later, Antoinette fell asleep in my arms and didn't budge when our daughter woke up. I shimmied out from under Antoinette and went to wake up the kids. This was the life I wouldn't trade for anything.

***

Want to read more from Lilly Grace Nash?

Love's Final Exoneration is the first book in the Brooklyn & Bennett, Attorneys-at-Law series.

When a man is wrongfully convicted of a brutal murder, Brooklyn Weston and Bennett Warren find themselves drawn into a case that will test the limits of their newfound partnership.

As they dig deeper, they uncover a web of corruption that reaches the highest levels of Monticello's justice system. With powerful forces working against them and time running out, Brooklyn and Bennett must risk everything to expose the truth and save an innocent man from a fate worse than death.

But in a town where lies masquerade as justice, will their love for each other and their commitment to the truth be enough to overcome the shadows of corruption?

Join Brooklyn and Bennett in this gripping romantic legal thriller that explores the depths of injustice and the heights of redemption. The fight for truth has never been more personal.

Don't miss out!

Visit the website below and you can sign up to receive emails whenever Lilly Grace Nash publishes a new book. There's no charge and no obligation.

https://books2read.com/r/B-A-WUJHB-XEGDF

BOOKS 2 READ

Connecting independent readers to independent writers.

Also by Lilly Grace Nash

Courting Justice
Alliances & Betrayals
The Billionaire's Legal Affair
Objection to Love
Love's Final Exoneration

SEALs of Love Romance
Undercover Hearts
Fractured Hearts
Healing Hearts

Second Chance Romance
Damaged Ex-SEAL's Second Chance
Ex-SEAL's Second Chance

Tides of Love: Military

Tides of Desire A Soldier's Canvas
Tides of Love Rhythms of Passion

Standalone
Billionaire's Nanny Fake Marriage
Silent Hearts, Secret Desires
Boss Daddy's Nanny

Watch for more at https://jllampublishing.com/
lilly-grace-nash.

About the Author

My name is Lilly Grace Nash. I was born and raised in a small town in rural Georgia. Growing up in this close-knit community, I developed a deep appreciation for the values and beauty of simple country life. But even more than that, I fell head over heels in love with the enchanting world of romance novels.

Read more at https://jllampublishing.com/lilly-grace-nash.